Thor:

A Paranormal Protector Tale

Book 1 in the Heart of Ice series

DEMELZA CARLTON

ONE

When he spotted the plain at the end of the pass, Thor couldn't help but grin. He quickened his step, eager to finally meet Jarl Erik's men in battle.

This was what they'd trained for. Planned for. Yearned for, since the day they'd returned home from a raid only to find Erik's handiwork. No one left alive, and the village still smouldering. And what Erik and his men had done to his sister, Sif…

Even now he had trouble banishing the image from his head. She'd looked like she'd been mauled by a beast. Deep gashes that slashed from her face down the chest of the tunic Thor had recognised as one of his own, slicing flesh and fabric so that she would have bled out from her wounds quickly, had they not killed her outright. And clutched in her hands, those cold, stiffened fingers not relinquishing their hold even in death, their father's hammer. Sif had fought with her last breath, Thor did not doubt, and was likely in Valhalla with all the other warriors right now, but she deserved more. She deserved justice.

Thor's thirst for vengeance had smouldered ever since. Finally, he could unleash the full fury of its flame on Erik and his men who had taken everything from him.

But even the crunch of his boots on the snow could not drown out the worried whispers of those who followed him.

"One of the scouts didn't come back."

"They could be waiting for us. Ready to

ambush us."

"What if…"

Indeed, what if?

Thor lifted his hammer high into the air. "What if, when we leave the pass, we come charging out of the snow and straight into battle? Oh, the glory of it. To fight and die in battle, to be reunited in Valhalla with those who died in Erik's cowardly attack on our village? Or to be victorious, and send Erik to Hel with all the other cowards?" He shook his hammer. "Onward to glory!"

"Onward!" came Odin's shout from higher up the pass. As well he might. He'd lost his wife and sons in the raid – he had more reason for vengeance than all the rest of them put together. "To victory!"

The other men picked up the cry, until it became one wordless shout that carried them all forward, boots no longer crunching but pounding, like the beat of a hundred drums, first at Thor's back and then on his flanks, as eager to enter battle as Thor himself.

If Erik didn't know they were coming, he knew now. Thor hoped the man quaked in his boots.

"For Odin and glory!" Thor swore as he raced out onto the plain.

And straight into the battle he'd prayed for.

He swung his hammer until it dripped with blood, and still the battle raged. For every man he felled, two more seemed to spring up in his place. Like some sort of sorcery.

"For Odin and glory!" he roared again, and he heard the answering call from far fewer men than before. He fought on with renewed vigour, for those who were already waiting in Valhalla.

Afternoon faded into twilight, and still he fought on. Another and another and another.

Then Erik's men seemed to pause, as though they'd heard a command he had not.

Had Erik ordered them to surrender or retreat, like the coward he was? Elation welled up in Thor's chest.

"For Odin!" he shouted, rushing forward

into the fray.

He was forced to halt, as Tyr and one of Erik's men blocked his way. Erik's man fell, and Tyr lifted his axe to deliver a killing blow…only for the most enormous wolf Thor had ever seen to fasten its jaws around Tyr's hand.

The axe dropped to the ground.

The creature reared up, extending its claws, and raked them down Tyr's front, before dragging them free from the dead man's flesh to unleash a fountain of blood. Tyr collapsed, sightless eyes staring up at the Valkyries no doubt coming to collect his soul to take to Valhalla, as the slashes on his face and chest wept his lifeblood into the snow.

Just like Sif…

"For Sif!" Thor roared, charging the creature.

Was it a wolf, or a man? Or some unholy union of both?

The creature rose up from four legs onto two, so that it stood taller than even Thor, and grinned. It was a wolfish grin, but the expression in its eyes was definitely human.

Whatever this thing was, it was an abomination. A monster that deserved to die. For Sif and Tyr and no doubt countless others it had slain.

Thor swung his hammer...

...but darkness enveloped him before he could land a blow on the beast.

TWO

"Ah, you must be the other Harald Medal winner."

Sibyl spun around, feeling dangerously like a turtle about to tip over, with her heavy pack still strapped to her back, until she sighted the woman who'd spoken and managed to steady herself against the wall.

She looked like she belonged here, all tall and blonde with broad shoulders that would have no problem with Sibyl's pack.

Sibyl wished her pack was a shell, so she could crawl inside and hide. She was definitely small enough to fit. Not like this Viking shieldmaiden.

Not for the first time, Sibyl wished one of her cousins were here. Or all of them. Tacey, who got along with everybody. Callie, who cursed everybody. Sometimes literally, even as she swore magic didn't exist. Octavia, who was Batman for computers while seeming to know every illegitimate businessperson in the Southern Hemisphere. Or even Alethea, who was too damn nice for her own good.

But none of them had won the Harald Medal, so all her cousins were back home in Western Australia, while she was on the other side of the world, almost in the Arctic Circle, no less, about to go on the archaeological dig of a lifetime. Three months ahead of schedule, thanks to global warming.

The Harald Medal was only awarded once every five years, and last time, they hadn't found a suitable candidate. So the odds of two medallists in the same place at the same time were practically astronomical, if not downright impossible.

The Viking woman grinned, like she was reading Sibyl's mind. "I know, right? I mean, last time they didn't pick anyone at all, so this time, having two winners is just weird. I did a bit of digging. It turns out the old guy whose company sponsors the medal – and his name isn't Harald, by the way, which surprised me – was in hospital five years ago, when the medal wasn't awarded, and he left the selection process up to his company board. They decided the financial outlay was more than they could afford, so to cut costs, they simply announced they didn't have anyone suitable. Fast forward five years. Not-Harald has happily recovered from heart surgery, and he's fired the board for making a mess of his company. To make up for the mess they made of the medal, this year he decided to have two winners. You…and me." She pressed a hand to her chest, then held it out for Sibyl to shake. "I'm Jorunn, by the way. I do reindeer."

Sibyl shook her hand, but now she was even more confused. "I'm Sibyl, and…wait, you do what?" She couldn't possibly do reindeer. Who said they were into bestiality when meeting someone for the first time?

Jorunn laughed. "Reindeer. Historic human-reindeer interactions, both hunting and domestication. At least, that's what I'm hoping to do my PhD project on, if we find enough evidence in the Jotunheimen Mountains this dig. Don't worry, I won't tread on your toes. You do Vikings, don't you?"

Sibyl felt her cheeks grow hot. She'd never done a Viking, or any man who looked like one. Sure, she might have a type, and Chris Hemsworth might tick all the boxes for it, but she'd never…

Jorunn didn't seem to be the least bit embarrassed. "Have you already sampled the local man candy? I swear, Norway is like Hemsworth heaven. I mean, sure, you can't check out the goods like on the beach back home, but Vikings sure are alive and well here. I wouldn't mind one myself, even if it's only for one night." She blinked. "Oh, but you're hoping for a dead one, aren't you? I thought that was what your project summary said…"

Sibyl cleared her throat and found her voice. "I'm hoping for evidence of a battle mentioned on a runestone found in a Viking grave a few years ago. The whole thing is pretty vague, and some scholars suggest it's referring to a myth about Thor and Loki in Utgard that never actually happened, but it also mentions a mountain pass that was also thought to be mythical…until one really warm summer revealed a whole bunch of artefacts right where the pass was supposed to be. My supervisor thinks that if there really is a two-thousand-year-old pass through this part of the Jotunheimen Mountains, and it's pretty clear from the surveys already done at the site that it was a rather busy highway in its time, it's possible this battle and the nearby village they were fighting over might have actually existed, too."

"Yep, dead Vikings. I'm not sure who's crazier – you or Karl – because you both want to find corpses."

"I don't need to find corpses. Just…evidence of the battle. Or the village. After a battle there are bodies, unless they burned them all, which surely they wouldn't have done to everyone, because the early Vikings believed that was a sign of honour, sending the slain to Valhalla, which they wouldn't have wanted for the losers, who they probably would have dumped in a mass grave, or at the feet of their own slain warriors. Even a village would have graves. Or some sign of the settlement. Weapons, foundations, midden heaps…something." Sibyl blew out a breath. "Sorry. I know the chances of finding anything are slim, and I'll probably have to rework my entire project to encompass whatever we do or don't find, but…it all just fits so well. Like something's out there, waiting to be found."

Sibyl ducked her head. Great. Now Jorunn probably thought she was an idiot. Or a conspiracy theorist. At least Sibyl hadn't mentioned the crazy theories involving aliens that the Marvel movies had only reinforced.

"Mm. Sounds like we'll be fighting over the arrowheads, if we find any." Jorunn didn't look pleased.

"Oh, no, of course not. Early Vikings rarely used bows and arrows in combat, except when they were defending the shore against raiders arriving by boat. I know sea levels have changed a lot over the years, but not at this altitude. Hunting, however…" She paused to think for a moment. "Really? Reindeer? I mean, I guess it's really just venison, but if any of the kids back home who still believe in Santa Claus knew people ate Rudolph…"

Jorunn grinned. "All the more reason for us to write research papers for peer reviewed journals and not children's books. With luck, we'll both get enough out of this survey to write a thesis on, and before we know it, we'll be picking our postdoctoral projects."

"Amen to that."

Jorunn dropped her voice to a whisper. "Anything's better than being stuck with…"

"Pah! PhD students! Worse than rats!" The sneering man who'd said it didn't look much older than they were. Early thirties at most. "I hope you two fifl don't expect special treatment. You'll be carrying your own gear, and don't expect a tent to yourself, either!"

Jorunn glared at him. "Who are you calling an idiot, idiot? You interrupted us discussing who gets which side of the tent. Right, roomie?" Jorunn linked her arm through Sibyl's.

Sibyl barely knew either of them, but she already knew who she'd prefer to share a tent with, so she just nodded and tried to look like none of this was news to her. Heaven knew she could do with a friend out here, with her family all back on the other side of the world.

He muttered something that didn't sound particularly nice as he stormed back out again.

"And that was…?" Sibyl prompted.

"Dr Nikolai Fridolfsen, newly minted PhD. He'll try to get you to call him Dr Fridolfsen, because he thinks he's the gods' gift to the world. Most people call him Nik, or Saint Nik, because he thinks the sun shines out of his arse. He's also the reason we have to share a tent, because there were enough until he joined the expedition." She stuck her tongue out at the door he'd departed through. "Of course, no one wants to share with him. He'll probably whine the whole time about how much better archaeology is in Egypt."

Sibyl couldn't help but feel a twinge of envy. Wasn't it every archaeologist's dream to do a dig in Egypt? "Is that where he did his PhD?"

Jorunn laughed. "Nope! He did his on a seventeen-hundred-year-old shirt found at the same site we're headed to. He was accepted for a postdoc in Egypt, but with all flights cancelled due to the pandemic, he never made it out there in time to join the survey team. They've been really lucky, too. They haven't made any of their findings public yet, but you wait…once it hits the news, everyone will know about it. Keep an eye out for Saqqara."

"How do you know all this stuff?" Sibyl asked.

Jorunn shrugged. "People talk. I listen. Besides, I had to catch a lift here with the rest of the team, and after fifteen minutes in a car with Nik, you'd wish he had gone to Egypt and opened a cursed tomb so he never made it back, too."

Sibyl couldn't condemn him as easily as Jorunn did. "Yeah, but…if I'd missed out on a paid research trip to Egypt because of the pandemic, I'd be pretty bitter about it, too. Anyone would. You've got to feel sorry for the guy."

Jorunn nodded slowly. "For the first ten minutes after you hear about it, before you meet him, maybe. Or maybe the first five minutes after you meet him. By the end of this week, you'll agree with me: it couldn't have happened to a nicer guy." She picked up her pack, which looked bigger than Sibyl's. "Come on, let's see if Lara needs any help loading up the supplies. According to Karl, there's always one bottle of aquavit too many to fit on the packhorses, and if you're there at the right time, with space in your pack, we'll have that bottle to toast our first night at site as roommates. What do you think?"

But before Sibyl could think, let alone reply, Jorunn led the way outside to where the packhorses waited. Yes, actual packhorses – the only way up into the mountains to the dig site, aside from their own two feet.

One thing was for certain: this was going to be an interesting trip.

THREE

Thor woke with a pounding head and a mouthful of swearing he couldn't spit out fast enough. What was that thing?

"I'll thank you to keep a civil tongue in your head, or I will no longer heal you. Then we'll see how long a man can live with a wound such as yours."

Thor's eyes flew open. Pain still lanced through his skull, but in the dimness, he could make out a feminine silhouette that was likely the source of the tart voice.

"Are you a witch?" he croaked. For surely only a woman with magic could heal him. He'd heard tales of witches who could work miracles and ones who could make a man's life a misery. Which one this woman was, he had yet to discover, but if she meant to heal him, he held onto hope that she might be the benevolent kind, for there was not much he could do if she meant him harm. His head had not hurt this much even after that night he'd challenged Loki to a drinking contest and drunk an entire barrel full of mead. He'd won the contest, but the next morning he had not felt like a victor.

This time, there had been no mead. Only a giant, grinning wolf man, with paws the size of his aching head…

"What was that thing?" he asked.

The witch, if that was what she was, pressed a hand to his forehead. "Hush. Healing requires focus, lest I knit your hair together instead of your wound, and I give you a hat you can never take off."

Definitely a witch, though a young one, by the sound of her voice. And comely, from what little he could see of her in the faint light.

"I am a mighty warrior. Many women have wanted me for their husband. If you heal me, and bring me back to fighting strength, I could make you the envy of all other women, and take you for my own," Thor offered.

"Mighty indeed. I've seen you fight. But you are still no match for Fenrir, so if you do not wish me to call on him to give you another blow to the head, you will hush and let me do my work. Father wants you well, but if I need to call for help to hold you down to heal you, he may decide you're more trouble than you're worth, and let Fenrir finish what he started."

Thor began to laugh. "That thing has a name? Fenrir?"

She set her hands on her hips. "He is as much a man as you, maybe more so, for he bested you in battle. If you are lucky, you may fight at his side next time. That is Father's wish, anyway." But it did not sound as if it was hers.

"And what is your wish?" Thor ventured. For if he could get her on his side, maybe…

"I wish men would not sneak up on settlements in the night to attack one another, so that we must fight to defend what is ours. I wish men could be content with what they have, instead of reaching for what is not theirs, wanting more. I wish you would shut your mouth so I can finish healing you and send you to the feast with Father like he wants, so that you will be his problem, and not mine."

Her hand pressed him down against the bed, and he yielded to her, for he suspected her patience was growing thin, and he did want her to heal him, if it was within her power. He was a fighter, and even he knew he could not fight while his head hurt.

Finally, she was done, dusting her hands off as if washing them of her responsibility for him. A pity, for she was pretty, even if she was a witch. Perhaps, if not for that creature's attack, he would not be wounded, and she would have admired him as the warrior he was. Women did flock to him, whether he willed it or no. Just not this witch. Thor sighed. Probably for the best. Comely or not, she had a sharp tongue, and he did not fancy her for a wife.

"Fenrir! He's ready to go see Father!" the girl called.

Thor braced himself for another attack from the beast, but instead he saw a man. A man much like himself, with the tall, broad stance of a warrior. This man, Thor knew he could best in a fight.

Then the man grinned, a wolfish smile that Thor feared would haunt his dreams for many years to come. For man or beast, this was the same creature he'd fought. Sif's killer. "Come on, little man. Thank Miss Astrid for her kindness in healing you instead of cutting out your heart, as you deserve." He held out his hand – yes, definitely a hand, and not a paw –

to help Thor up.

It rankled to be reminded of his courtesies by this creature, so Thor ignored the hand and rose to his feet unaided.

He might not like the witch's killer companion, but Thor was grateful to the girl. Especially now he could stand, with his head no longer hurting. A miracle indeed. He bowed to her. "My thanks to you, Miss Astrid. If you ever have need of my hammer, you have only to say the word, and I shall defend you."

He glanced around, but there was no sign of his hammer anywhere in the small cottage.

Fenrir saw him looking, and laughed. "A pretty pledge, though hardly necessary. You and your hammer are the property of Jarl Erik now. King Erik, if he has his way. And he will if none are strong enough to stand against him." A look passed between Fenrir and Astrid, before she ducked her head and looked away. "Come, little man. If you make a good impression on Erik at the feast, he may even give you your hammer back."

Thor followed Fenrir out of the cottage.

"Fenrir…"

Fenrir halted. "Yes, Miss Astrid?" His entire stance was expectant, hopeful. What did a creature like him hope for?

"Don't hurt him. I'd hate to have to heal him all over again. It was hard enough work the first time."

Disappointment flickered over Fenrir's face for only a moment, and then it was gone. "As you wish, Miss Astrid. Your wish is my command, of course." There was no mockery in his words.

Thor wondered if his subservience was because the girl was a witch, or because she was Jarl Erik's daughter. Curious that she had not issued the same command to Thor as she had to Fenrir. Did the girl mean to make it easier for Thor to have his vengeance for Sif's murder, in forbidding Fenrir to fight back? For the moment Thor had his hammer back, the wolf man's life was forfeit. This Thor swore.

"Whatever you think you know, you are

wrong, little man," Fenrir said softly as they moved away from the cottage. "Forget Miss Astrid, for you have taken up enough of her time. If you so much as look at her again, I will kill you, no matter what her father says. Jarl Erik may rule Utgard and all of these lands, but it is Miss Astrid I am sworn to serve, which I will do to my last breath. Which will come long after yours, I promise you."

Fenrir flashed a grin, and for a moment, Thor thought there were more fangs than teeth in the man's mouth. A wolfish smile indeed.

So Jarl Erik commanded a witch and a wolf. That explained the sorcery on the battlefield, as well as this beast. If the man was so powerful, could anyone stand against him?

It was Thor's turn to grin. He'd never been one to back down from a battle, even if he was the last man standing from the raiding party that had come through the pass. The moment Erik gave him his hammer back, Thor would show both Erik and Fenrir what a true warrior was.

FOUR

"You know, you really should try the porridge one day. A hot breakfast does wonders for you when you're working in the snow all day," Lara said, ladling out a bowl for Jorunn. The site manager reminded Sibyl of Tacey, the way she took care of everyone, or tried to.

Sibyl scrunched up her nose. "No thanks. I lived with my cousin when she was introducing her baby girl to solids, and we spent months pretending to like all kinds of mush so she'd eat it. I like my cornflakes with plenty of crunch, even if it's with powdered milk. I have my coffee. That's hot enough for me." She held up her cup in a toast to morning caffeine, the miracle drug that got everyone going, even when it was minus ten outside, like today.

Jorunn laughed so hard she almost snorted her porridge. "Sounds like enough to put you off having kids for life. Is that why you're here, doing your PhD a world away from there? To escape your family, like me?"

Homesickness smote Sibyl hard. "No. I love my family, and my cousins. Even Rory, who's five now, and at school. I'm here because…" Because she'd always had her family around. Mum, or her cousins. Out here, without them, she had to do stuff for herself. Make her mark, a mark that was hers alone. "Because I want to do something that's just me, alone."

Jorunn grinned as she reached for an apple. "So you joined an expedition with a whole team of us, so you can't possibly do anything alone?" She dropped her voice into a pretty good approximation of Karl, the expedition leader. "Safety first, never go alone!"

Even Lara laughed at that. "He's right, though. Never leave camp alone. There are wolves and bears in these mountains, and you don't want to meet a wolverine, either. Unless it's Hugh Jackman. That man could share my tent any time."

"Ah, if we're talking Aussie actors, I'd prefer a Hemsworth over Hugh. Right, Sibyl?" Jorunn asked. She tossed her empty porridge bowl in the washing up tub and bit into her apple.

Sibyl felt her cheeks grow hot. "I came all the way over here for a real Viking, not some Aussie bloke pretending to be one."

Jorunn laughed again. "Oh, that's right! But if you do find a Viking body in the ice, you are not bringing him into our tent. Even if he is hotter than a Hemsworth, I draw the line at necromancy."

Sibyl choked on her cornflakes. "Don't you

mean necrophilia? Necromancy is raising the dead. Necrophilia is sleeping with them."

"No to either of them, especially in our tent. Then again…if you raised him from the dead, he's not really dead, and if he's still hot, would it really be necrophilia? Theoretically…"

Sibyl smacked her arm. "Now who's considering sleeping with a corpse? We'd have to find one first, and even Karl thinks that's unlikely. But he still brought the body bag, just in case."

Jorunn tossed her apple core in the bin and headed back to the washing up tub to do her dishes. "Everybody wants to be the one to find the holy grail. Don't tell me you don't want to find one of Hemsworth's ancestors under the ice."

Nik stormed into the mess tent and slammed his mug down next to the pot of hot water. "What is wrong with you Australian girls? Always you are wanting to find that actor man here, when you will not find anything at all unless you keep your mind on your work!

This is not the place to find bodies. For proper human remains to study, you must go to Egypt, where even the ancients knew how to preserve a body properly, instead of by accident like these primitive Vikings!" He let out a string of words that sounded like swearing, before stomping out of the tent, slopping coffee over his boots and swearing some more.

Sibyl turned to find Jorunn's eyes on her. "Are you still feeling sorry for him?" Jorunn asked.

"We had a pool in the office, to see how long it would take before one of his colleagues in Egypt shut him in a pyramid or something," Lara said. "Ah, we all wish he'd gone!"

Sibyl sighed. She rarely wished ill of people, but after a week of working with Saint Nik, she had to admit, "If I was working on the same dig in Egypt as him, and I knew about your pool, I would have volunteered to do it, even if he only stayed stuck in there for an hour or so."

"Only an hour or so? A thousand years is too good for him! Imagine archaeologists a thousand years from now, finding him and thinking he's a tomb robber!" Jorunn said.

"Fifteen minutes until we start the survey, girls, so what's on the cards for today? To win your chance of no dishes at dinnertime…" Lara paused for effect. "What do you bet we'll find?"

"Arrows," Jorunn said promptly, like she did every day. She'd already won twice this week.

Sibyl thought for a moment. Every other day she'd been wrong, so what was one more? "A Viking sex god I can raise from the dead who can sleep in Nik's tent, and whack him with his axe every time he snores."

Lara laughed so hard she spat out her coffee. "Oh, I'd pay to see that!"

So would Sibyl, she thought but didn't say.

FIVE

The scents of smoke and roasted meat greeted Thor before he even entered the longhouse. He'd heard the shouts of merriment from inside and dismissed them as normal eventide fare in any Viking camp. Only now did realisation dawn on him that for Erik and his men, this was a victory feast.

A victory over Odin's men.

Thor's blood ran cold. He was no berserker,

but as his rage built with every step toward the longhouse, he fancied he was fuelled with enough fury to take down a dozen men, maybe more, the moment he held his hammer in his hands again. Or even just an axe…

His gaze dropped to Fenrir's belt, only to see for the first time that the man carried no weapons at all. Like he was merely a lowly thrall instead of a mighty warrior who'd bested Thor himself in a fight. Nothing about this wolf man made sense. Not that it needed to. He would be the first to die, as Sif's shade demanded.

Fenrir entered the longhouse, with Thor hot on his heels. Not a single head turned in their direction. There was no fanfare, and no one announced his arrival. Thor wasn't sure whether to be insulted by their disregard or relieved, for entering their victory feast as Erik's prisoner would surely have them jeering instead of cheering at him. But to be ignored completely was not something Thor was used to.

Fenrir merely shrugged and pushed his way through the crowd, taking a seat in a dark corner, far from the fire. Again, like a thrall.

But Thor did not intend to shrink away into the shadows. He'd come to confront Erik for his crimes against his people, and if Thor was the sole survivor of his village, then by all that was holy, he would do so, even if it cost him his life. Sif's shade demanded it.

So he stood and waited.

Waited while Erik's men crowded around the high table, hooting and cheering at what appeared to be a contest between two men over who could eat the fastest…or perhaps the most, Thor wasn't sure. Servants kept bringing more meat, bread and mead to the table, as the two men consumed it all.

More of Erik's beastly warriors, Thor told himself, curling his lip in disgust. At least the wolf had been a warrior. These two gluttons were more like wild boars, or pigs, the way they ate.

Erik himself looked on from his chair,

clapping his hands in approval as one of the men downed a horn of mead, before seizing a fresh joint of meat. The mead drinker bore a distinct resemblance to Erik – a son, perhaps?

The other man glanced up at Erik's son, then Erik himself, before grim determination wrinkled his brow as he, too, reached for more meat.

Thor started in surprise. What was Loki doing, seated at Erik's high table? He'd been the best of Odin's scouts, the sneakiest snake who could find a way in and out of anywhere. Thor hadn't seen him during the battle, but that hadn't been surprising, for people rarely saw Loki until he'd already struck a blow, and by then it was too late. They'd been brothers in arms for as long as Thor could remember, and they were brothers still, if Loki had somehow survived the battle.

Together, they would take on Erik and all his warriors.

After Loki had won this contest, for surely Erik would not appreciate Loki embarrassing his son.

Yet Loki was flagging, whilst the son's appetite seemed to grow. The world seemed to shift as Thor realised Loki was going to lose.

Erik rose from his chair with a roar and declared his son the winner, amid cheers from the rest of his men. Loki, on the other hand, seemed to shrink in his seat, shoulders hunched over as he drank down his disappointment with a mug of mead.

"You! Hammer man!" Erik shouted, pointing at Thor.

The hall fell silent, the crowd parting so that Thor could see not only Erik, but the table in front of him, where his hammer lay.

"Your brother has accepted his place in my hall. How will you entertain us, and earn your place here, hammer man?" Erik demanded.

Now all eyes turned to Thor.

Thor considered correcting Erik. While he and Loki might look alike, they were not blood brothers. Indeed, Loki was usually the first to say something when someone made such a mistake. But after losing the contest, Loki seemed to want to avoid notice as much as possible, so Thor let Erik's words pass unchallenged.

For he had a challenge of his own to issue.

Thor looked Erik in the eye. "I would have my hammer back, Jarl Erik, and I challenge you to a drinking contest for it. He who can drink the most and stay standing will be the winner, before all these witnesses." He waved a hand at Erik's assembled warriors, who all held their breath. Evidently, it wasn't often that Erik himself was challenged beneath his own roof.

But Erik either did not notice the insult, or did not care. He laughed. "A drinking contest we shall have. The first to the bottom of the barrel who is still standing, then."

Servants brought forth two barrels, which were broached before them. Erik's barrel was placed beside his chair, so that he might easily dip a mug into it without rising. Thor was not offered the courtesy of a seat, and he had to steal a rough wooden cup from a passing servant instead of being offered a mug or drinking horn. No matter. When Thor had his hammer back, they would all pay for their poor hospitality.

"For Odin," he whispered as he drained the first cup. Odin was no doubt in Valhalla with his family, as he deserved, and Thor would join him soon enough.

A second cup chased the first, burning its way down Thor's gullet. A wiser man might have eaten something first, but Thor had no desire for food. No, all he wanted was vengeance for Sif. For Odin. And for all the rest of their village, murdered by these men.

Thor lifted a third cup, as an offering to the gods that they might grant him victory.

That's when he saw his gesture mirrored by a man in a dark corner of the hall. A man with a leather patch over one eye, so Thor did not recognise him at first, but he blinked and he knew. Odin had survived the battle, too, though he'd lost an eye doing so. He had no appetite, either. All he held was a rough cup of wine, raised in anticipation of Thor's victory.

A fourth cup, then a fifth. One after the other, Thor drank as if his life depended on it, for he suspected it did.

Something clattered to Thor's right. Loki had dropped his mug, which rolled across the table and onto the floor. Empty, for he'd drunk it all, and likely more besides, for Loki slumped to the table.

A ruse, Thor was sure of it. Loki was never beaten. He must only be pretending to be overcome by the feast. When Thor reclaimed his hammer, Loki would leap up, alert as ever, to fight by his side.

Thor lifted a sixth cup to his lips, and his eyes went to Odin. Odin slumped against the wall, almost sliding off the bench, as his cup slipped from his fingers.

Thor dipped his cup into the barrel for the seventh time. Except…was it one cup, or two? Or perhaps three? No…one, two, three…four? He'd never been so woozy before after drinking so little. Especially with Erik matching him drink for drink.

"I will challenge any man here to beat me in a race!" a reedy voice piped up.

Thor blinked. It couldn't be. Was that…Thialfi? How had the boy survived the battle?

"No man is faster than me!" Thialfi declared. "On a count of three. One, two, three!" He bolted for the door.

No one followed him.

Thor allowed himself to smile. Thialfi might escape, and live a good, long life.

Thialfi made it to the doorway, before he appeared to trip over something and pitched forward. Thor expected him to catch himself, or at least rise and try to run again, but the boy stayed down.

A man with a bow in one hand marched over to Thialfi and reached down. With one mighty yank, he brandished a bloodied arrow. An arrow bearing Thialfi's blood, Thor realised.

Thialfi did not rise because the boy was dead. The bowman had been faster than the boy. Thor closed his eyes. All the more reason to beat Erik in this drinking contest. To win his hammer back and…and…

Loki lay face down on the table. Odin had slid to the floor, where he was now snoring. And Erik lifted a horn of ale to his lips, curling them into a knowing smile.

"The drink…you drugged it. You are an honourless wolverine, as much a beast as any of your so-called men. Give me back my weapon and I shall take on all of you. Show you what a real warrior can do!" Thor growled, reaching for his hammer. Or what he thought was his hammer, for there seemed to be half a dozen of the things lying on the table, but when his hand closed around what should have been the handle, he grasped only air.

Then Thor hit the ground, so all he could see was the soot-blackened beams of the roof.

Erik's face swam into view. "You couldn't best my own grandmother or even her cat in a fight. You don't belong in Valhalla, hammer man."

An old woman's face peered at him. And was that…a cat? Thor had never seen a butter coloured cat before, yet there it was, looking down upon him as though he were the lowliest thrall to ever crawl out of a midden.

"He drank three times as much as the others before he succumbed, Erik. This one's stronger than the rest. He will make a fine fighter in your army, just like I told you."

Thor opened his mouth to tell her that he'd rather die than fight for the man who murdered his sister, but darkness swallowed him before he could get a word out.

SIX

"That's not how you record the GPS!"

"But that's how I've always been taught…"

"This is a real archaeology dig, not some student exercise in a fifty-year-old rubbish dump!"

"Actually, I did my honours on an eight-thousand-year-old site near the Burrup Peninsula back home. One of the first underwater Aboriginal sites ever investigated and…"

"You call this documentation? Karl's two-year-old granddaughter has better handwriting than this!"

Sibyl peered at the page. "Actually, that's one of yours. You borrowed my blue pen when you forgot to bring anything of your own to write with, Nik. And you didn't give it back, either."

"That's Doctor Fridolfsen, girl!"

Sibyl hadn't wanted to punch anyone so much in her life. Or knee him in the groin. She wished there had never been any pandemic, and Saint Nik had gone to Egypt like he'd planned, so he'd be someone else's problem.

"You'll never get your PhD with substandard work like this! It's a wonder you even got your degree at all. Of course, pretty girls have an advantage. You must have slept with your professors. No other explanation."

Tears of anger burned Sibyl's eyes. Callie, her cousin, had been one of her teachers, and she'd said she'd never had a student who'd learned Norse runes faster than Sibyl. Sibyl had been invited up to the Burrup because they'd needed an extra person to process all the artefacts, and she'd been recommended for the job by no less than two of her unit coordinators.

But Saint Nik wouldn't listen to a word of it. He'd probably accuse her of sleeping with them, too.

She wished Callie were here to cast a curse on Nik. Something really horrible and creative, like having him catch some ancient disease that had melted out of the ice, which made his dick shrivel up and fall off. Or make him smell like a female reindeer in heat, so all the boy reindeer chased him around, trying to molest him…

"If you don't push him off a glacier before the season ends, I swear I will."

Sibyl glanced up, to find Jorunn watching her with a sympathetic smile on her face.

"Maybe he's right, and I don't belong here. It's not like we've found anything even remotely connected to Utgard. Whereas you've found two hunting arrows already…" Sibyl began.

"Three. Found a third one this morning," Jorunn said smugly. "Three arrows in two weeks is a new record, Karl said."

Sibyl sighed. "If the borders weren't closed, I'd give up and go home to Australia. I'm not cut out for this."

Jorunn's smile died. "Don't talk like that." She slung an arm around Sibyl's shoulder. "We're the first ever dual Harald Medal winners. The only two in a decade. Hundreds of candidates entered, and they picked us. We're the best there is. Saint Nik never won a medal. He's just jealous, not to mention bitter that it's our prize money that's funding this entire expedition. He wouldn't even be here if it weren't for us. We've only been out here two weeks. I bet your Buggerup dig didn't find anything in the first two weeks, either. We've got three arrows, and a bunch of other stuff."

Sibyl managed a smile. "Burrup, not

Buggerup. And yeah, it took them three years of underwater survey work to find a site as rich as the one they finally did locate."

"Maybe we should push Saint Nik in the lake, and see if he finds anything interesting there."

That didn't sound like a bad idea. Better than pushing him off a glacier, anyway. Then again, if he couldn't swim…

"He'd probably make us do his laundry while he sulks in his tent until his gear is dry. Or insist on borrowing our gear instead," Sibyl said.

Jorunn looked glum. "And he wouldn't wash it before he gave it back, either. Imagine having to wear your gear after he'd sweated in it for days, unwashed. Just kill me now."

"Only if you'd do the same for me," Sibyl quipped. God, it must be a bad day if she was making a death pact with her roommate before noon.

"Or…I could help you wish the dishes tonight, after dinner, and when everyone's gone to bed, you could help me liberate a bottle of Lara's aquavit and we could share it in the tent later. What do you say?" Jorunn asked.

Sibyl wanted to say yes, but… "You found an arrow today. That means you've won a night off doing the dishes. Plus…aren't those bottles all we have for the whole trip? What if Lara notices one missing?"

Jorunn shrugged. "They're for medicinal purposes. If she asks, I'll tell her Saint Nik was sapping our will to live, and nothing would restore it except some water of life. She'll understand. Besides, with the expedition budget higher than usual, we have a regular supply run. Jakop and his horses will be back in no time, and she can always order more for the next trip."

It sounded like a plan, and a good one. With all of her family so far away, Sibyl would be lost without Jorunn. "All right, then," she said.

"Ah, the day's not even half over. Who knows? This afternoon, we might find one of

Hemsworth's ancestors, complete with a hammer as big as he is, and he'll take one look at Saint Nik and pound him so deep into a glacier, no one will find him for a hundred years."

Sibyl had to smile at that one. "I think you're thinking of Captain America. He's the one who vanished beneath the Arctic ice and woke up much later."

"But he was a hot blonde dude, right?"

Sibyl laughed. "Yeah, he was that, too."

Jorunn didn't seem fazed. "Well, that's what they do with superhero movies, isn't it? They mash up all the stories into one movie-length one? So who says we won't find Thor holding his hammer, ready to jump to defend your reputation as an archaeologist? Maybe if we drink enough aquavit, he will!"

For a moment, anything seemed possible. Then a cloud slid in front of the sun, and the lake waters turned ashen grey again. Sibyl sighed. "All right, all right. Dishes and drinks tonight, whether we find something amazing or nothing at all. Deal?"

"Only if you promise not to talk about leaving again. You're the only one keeping me sane out here," Jorunn said.

"It's a deal," Sibyl said.

"Right, back to work," Jorunn said, taking her place at Sibyl's side, ready for another search pattern.

Where they might find anything, Sibyl told herself, as they began again.

SEVEN

Never…drinking…mead…again, Thor swore to himself in time with the deafening drumbeat in his head. This had to be Loki's fault. He never drank this much without Loki goading him into it.

Faint memories of Loki lying facedown on a table drifted through his sore head. Which had to mean Thor had won again, hadn't he? Then why did his head pound so?

Come to think of it, why was it so cold? No matter how much he'd had to drink, Thor would never be stupid enough to run naked in the snow. Yet it felt like a faint breeze tickled his bare chest, as he lay on something equally cold and hard, as glacier meltwater trickled through his veins. All that was nothing compared to the bite of a slab of ice landing on his chest, ice so cold it froze his heart solid.

Thor opened his mouth to scream at the white-hot pain, but no sound came out.

"The sacrifice is complete. He is now a protector who awaits my call."

Thor knew that voice. It belonged to the witch girl. Witch girl…what was her name?

Miss Astrid, his sluggish thoughts reminded him, along with the name of the abomination that guarded her: Fenrir the wolf man, murderer of Sif and countless others, under the command of Jarl Erik. Who still lived and breathed.

No. Thor had to end him. For Sif. He strained and struggled, but no matter what he did, he could not move.

"Protector Thor, what will you do when you hear my call?" the witch asked.

Thor's eyes flew open, and he could see her. She was younger than he was.

"I will answer your call, and fight at your command, mistress," Thor heard himself say, even as his head screamed at him not to.

"Will you protect me?" she asked.

"I am yours to command, mistress," Thor said.

A cold weight landed on his chest, before someone took his hand and laid it atop the icy metal. His hammer. If he could but grasp the handle and swing it, he could take out half a dozen of these men with one blow. More, maybe.

But he could not move his hand from the head of the hammer, let alone grip the handle.

"It is done. Bury him," the witch instructed.

Wait…what? Bury him?

Thor wanted to scream, to struggle, to fight, but he couldn't move as men surrounded him and lifted him, then lowered him. Down,

down…into a grave easily as deep as he was tall. Then the men stepped away, and for a moment, Thor saw the dusky sky, before a shadow peered down.

Fenrir, the abomination.

Thor tried to roar out a challenge to the wolf man, to grab the hammer and leap out of the grave they'd dug for him, to go down fighting, as was his right as a Viking warrior, but he could neither move nor make a sound.

"Sleep, protector, until you hear my call," the witch said.

A shower of soil and snow came down on him, followed by a hail of stones, until Thor could no longer see any light.

Then the water came, gushing down over the stones and soil and snow, soaking him. But it didn't stop there. The water level kept rising, and rising, until it covered his face, and he could no longer draw breath. Screaming silently, he surrendered to the darkness once more.

But not willingly. Never that.

EIGHT

Sibyl wasn't sure what was worse – the hangover from drinking too much aquavit with Jorunn last night, or the porridge Lara had insisted she eat to combat the hangover, which now swirled in her stomach, threatening to come right back up again and splatter across the rocks. The rocks she was supposed to be surveying for artefacts…

She rested a hand on the rock cairn she

knew dated back over a thousand years – it had been surveyed at length on an earlier dig. As long as she didn't knock it over, no one would mind if she took a quick break to get her stomach contents under control. She was never eating porridge ever again. Goldilocks could keep the foul gloop.

Now her vision was playing tricks on her. The rocks in front of her looked lighter than the others, like someone had parked a car on them when it was raining, leaving the stone beneath bone dry, while the rest was damp and dark. Then another lighter patch, a couple of metres further along, and a third patch, too. Very small cars, though. Only a couple of metres long and barely a metre wide. More like someone had laid their swag tents on these three spots, instead of cars. Which was crazy, because this whole area was loose rock on top of permafrost, and trying to sleep on a surface like that was more like something out of the princess and the pea…only the whole surface was peas, and the peas were fist sized and sharp.

She scuffed her boot at the nearest patch of pale rock, dislodging a couple, before a third came up with part of a broken sheet of ice. Like someone had poured water here and it had frozen in a sheet beneath the stones…

Sibyl kicked aside a few more rocks, revealing more and more of the ice sheet, until she'd revealed it all. Yes, the ice sheet was about as big as a swag…but it had melted in the warm weather, so it was thin enough to break when she tapped it with her marker sticks.

Well, if she really wanted to see what lay under the ice…

Sibyl poked the bundle of sticks under the nearest edge of the ice sheet, slowly working it deeper underneath it until it was about as far as it could go. Then she put her weight to the lever, pushing with all her strength to flip the sheet over. It took a couple of tries, especially as the sheet kept breaking, until she finally managed to shift that, too.

Only to find another layer of ice, which

didn't shatter the way the first one had when she tapped it. In fact, it almost sounded like metal…

Throwing the sticks aside, she raked her boot across the ice. Yep, that was metal, all right. Almost as big as her boot, and glinting in the sun. She tried to dig around it with her gloved hands, but whatever it was, it was stuck firmly in the ice.

"Guys, I think I found something," she called to the rest of the team, who'd continued walking their transects without realising she'd fallen behind.

Nik said something Sibyl was certain was a swear word in Norwegian. "Just put a flag in it and keep moving. You're holding us up." He turned his back on her and kept going.

The others didn't dismiss her so easily.

"What is it?" Karl asked eagerly.

"Something big and metal," Sibyl shouted back.

She saw his shoulders sag as if he was disappointed. Of course, it was no secret Karl wanted to find his own ice man.

But he planted his marker sticks in the spot where he'd ended his survey, and trudged back to where Sibyl knelt.

"The rocks looked lighter than the ones around it, so I shifted a few, and found an ice sheet underneath, so I moved that, too," Sibyl said, pointing. "And under it was this."

Karl dropped to his knees beside her and pulled out his canteen. He unscrewed the lid, then carefully poured the contents over the artefact and the surrounding ice.

A wisp of steam rose up, then vanished.

Sibyl dared to look down again, and gasped.

Whatever it was had been intricately carved or forged in…

"Jelling style," Karl breathed, in almost the same moment as Sibyl thought it. "See the swirling and intertwining, with the heads in profile? You know how old this is?"

"At least a thousand years," Sibyl said, barely believing it.

"It looks like an axe, but something this

ornate would never have been used as a weapon. We'll have to dig it out of the ice to see," Karl said.

By day's end, they'd all carried pan after pan of warm water over to the site and dumped it on the axe head, which turned out to still have its haft, too, bound in leather. By the time they stopped for dinner, they'd melted enough ice to chip the weapon out of its glacial grave, so they could place it and the not inconsiderable amount of ice still encrusting it into a tray where it might melt overnight in the warmth of the mess tent.

Sibyl barely tasted her dinner. She couldn't keep her eyes off her axe, though she knew it wasn't really hers. But she had found it, and it was from the right period, and it definitely wasn't something used in hunting. Not something that ornate.

She scraped the bottom of the bowl, only to discover she'd eaten it all. Time to wash up, then.

But when Sibyl picked up the sponge, Lara

shook her head. "You called that find. You're not doing the washing up tonight."

Sibyl could only laugh. "I did not predict that we'd find a ceremonial axe today."

"No, you said Thor's hammer. And that's no axe."

Sibyl's eyes followed Lara's gaze to the tray where the find lay in a pool of water. Sure enough, the ice had sheared away from the axe head, which was bigger and heavier than she'd first thought. And while it was shaped like an axe, where an axe might have a blade was too thick and blunt – more like a hammer or a mace.

"Oh my God, you really found Thor's hammer!" Jorunn exclaimed, hugging Sibyl from behind.

Sibyl couldn't respond. She could only stand there stiffly and stare.

NINE

Sibyl's mind spun with plans. First, they'd need to completely melt the ice off the weapon and catalogue the find in detail, with more photographs. Then, they'd need to get it to one of the university labs and do some scans. X-ray and CT scans, for a start. The metal was shinier than she'd expect for a thousand-year-old Viking weapon, which were mostly iron. She'd have expected such a weapon to be more rusty than this was, which meant she'd have to find a way to analyse the metal. The handle looked like leather wrapped around wood, and identifying the species might require DNA analysis, which she'd never had to do before, so she'd need to look up relevant papers…

"So, what's the plan for tomorrow?" Lara asked. "Finish the transects, or see if there's anything else buried beneath the ice where Sibyl found Thor's hammer?"

Sibyl's whirling mind stopped dead. "There might be more than just the hammer?" she blurted out.

Nik made a derisive sound. "You are still expecting your Australian actor man? Foolish girl. If such a weapon were buried as grave goods, the body will be little more than a skeleton now. Not to mention it's solid ice. All that work likely for nothing more than a few bones? I say we continue the transects, and see if we can find something of importance."

Karl eyed Nik.

For a moment, Sibyl wondered if Karl was actually going to tell Nik off for being such an arsehole.

"If the hammer is part of someone's grave goods, it's likely there'll be far more than bones in there with him. A warrior who carried such a weapon would definitely be rich and important. The hammer might just be the start," Karl said.

Of course Karl would see the research possibilities above all else, even Nik being a complete dick to everyone else on the team. But even Sibyl couldn't be upset at the possibility of finding more. A warrior's grave would be an amazing find, and more than enough to write one if not several research papers on. Besides, if a battle really had occurred here, then he wouldn't be the only warrior who'd died, and there would be other graves. Maybe this was what she'd come here to find.

Karl continued, "So we should probably mark that site for further investigation later in the season, when the ice has melted some more. What's the weather forecast for tomorrow?"

Lara tugged the satellite phone out of its cradle and frowned at it. A long moment passed before she said, "Well, that answers that. Early snowfall forecast for tomorrow, with more snow and freezing temperatures for the rest of the week. That ice won't be melting any time soon. When the weather clears, we'd be better off returning to transects."

Sibyl's hopes soared, then plummeted. She was on the cusp of discovering the site of Utgard, only to be stopped by a bloody snow storm. That'd never happen in Australia, or at least not at any of the sites she'd worked at.

Well, there had been cyclone alerts at Burrup, but bad storms could happen anywhere, and you usually had enough warning that a storm was coming to put in a few extra hours a day while the good weather lasted, then protect the site as best you could before you had to evacuate as the bad weather came in. It was sort of a standard joke among the Burrup team that there was always time for one more dive.

Surely there was time to go out to look at the site after dinner, just in case they'd missed something…

Karl rose. "All right, time for an early night, everyone. It's been a busy week, and I couldn't be more pleased at how much we've surveyed so far. With bad weather moving in overnight, everyone's to stay in camp until Lara gives us the all clear. It couldn't come at a better time. Jakop's due to arrive with another load of supplies in a day or two, so I want all our finds properly documented so we can send everything back to the lab with him. Everything done by the end of the day tomorrow, people!" He headed out.

Sibyl's feet carried her after him, almost of their own volition. "Are you sure we shouldn't take one last look at the hammer site before it's covered by snowfall?" she asked. "I mean, we melted a lot of ice, but we were more focussed on getting the hammer out than seeing if there was anything else with it. What if…?"

Karl shook his head. "The temperature's already dropping. Any ice we melted will have frozen already, preserving any finds for us until it's warmer, later in the season. Don't worry. Whatever's there has waited a thousand years to be found. Another few months won't make much difference."

If she'd waited a thousand years to be found, she'd be pissed about being made to wait even longer. "But…"

He held up his hand. "I want to find out what's in there as much as you do. Maybe even more, because if it really is a grave, this could be the ice mummy we've been hoping for. But that's even more reason to wait until the ice melts on its own, because the lower the temperature, the less damage there'll be to the body before we can dig it out and transport it to the lab for analysis. Helicopters can't fly in bad weather, and even if it could, there'd be nowhere safe to land it until later in the season.

"But it doesn't matter what's in there, or what the flying conditions are. We filed a risk management plan with the university to allow this expedition, and our safety procedures don't allow survey work outside the camp after dark or during a snowstorm. Besides, I know I need to get my documentation complete. Is all of yours done?"

Sibyl felt her cheeks redden. "Well, no…" Mostly because Nik had driven her out of the mess tent with accusations of incompetence and bad handwriting so many times, that she'd been waiting for a chance to do it when he wasn't around. Problem was, he'd always been around, so she hadn't had a chance. She probably should have tried to do it in the tent she shared with Jorunn instead, but Jorunn always seemed to have something fun to talk about, or to drink, or both, and after a couple of shots of aquavit, Sibyl knew better than to try to write anything legible.

"Good. See that you get plenty of rest

tonight, and take care of paperwork tomorrow. It helps to develop good fieldwork practice early on, so that by the time you're my age and leading expeditions, it's just automatic. One less thing to worry about when you're making a dozen decisions a minute and everyone defers to you." He nodded to her, wished her good night, and headed off to his tent.

Sibyl stared after him, half annoyed and half…gratified, or at least she thought that's what it was. For all Nik's insults, Karl seemed to think she had what it took for a lifelong career in archaeology, up to and including leading expeditions in the future.

God, she wished she could talk to her cousins right now. Okay, Callie would probably offer to curse someone, even if only Nik actually deserved it, and Octavia could probably offer half a dozen solutions of questionable legality, depending on who she'd been doing IT support for lately, and none of that would be particularly helpful. It was Tacey she really wanted to talk to – because Tacey had always been the mama bear of Bell House, with the right advice at any time, no matter what the problem was.

So, what would Tacey say?

Sibyl took a deep breath and blew it out. Tacey would say that Karl was right and Nik was wrong. If she just focussed on the project in front of her, and did her best work on that, the future would take care of itself, and she didn't need to worry about that right now.

But the project in front of her was Thor's hammer, or whoever's hammer it was, and the site where they'd found it. Which wasn't actually that far outside their camp boundaries…

Besides, it wasn't even full dark yet. The days were getting longer, and the sun had only just set. There was still plenty of light in the sky. If she wandered over to the site now and just had a quick look before the meltwater froze over, then she'd know for sure if there was anything else to be found. Anything still under the ice could stay there, but if they'd missed something while they were extracting the hammer, she'd never forgive herself if it got damaged between now and later in the season.

Nobody knew safety procedures better than she did – a product of mostly working at sites sponsored by mining companies back in Western Australia. She'd done so many Take 5 checks before starting work, she could probably get a job as a safety officer on a mine site back home, if archaeology wouldn't pay the bills.

Then again, the best way to pay the bills was to find something to write plenty of papers on, to show the world she really did deserve the Harald Medal, and more besides.

She'd just be taking a walk, to help her think, Sibyl told herself. If Karl caught her, she'd just say she'd been lost in thought, and not realised she'd walked outside the camp boundaries on her way back from the bathroom tent.

Now she wished she'd kept her boots on,

instead of changing into her camp slippers for dinner. If she detoured via her tent, she might have time to swap shoes…

Not if she wanted to use the remaining daylight.

Sibyl nodded. Yes, she was sure now. Tacey would tell her to do her best work on what was in front of her. Which meant one last check of the hammer site, just to make sure.

Without looking back, she marched off into the sunset.

TEN

HELP. Thor, help me.

Thor reached for his hammer before his eyes were even fully open.

That call. That voice. He had to help her. He'd sworn to serve, and serve he would.

Just…needed…hammer…

He would fight to defend her with his last breath. No matter what the cost, or who the foe was. Maybe even the wolf man…

Just…needed…his hammer…

Thor reached for it, where he knew it would be.

Where it should be.

Only to grasp at empty air…

ELEVEN

Sibyl swore as the stubbed her toe for the third time. Even with a headtorch in the dusky light, it was hard to see where she was going, and every rock looked the same. She really should have stopped to grab her boots. But now she was here, she might as well take a look at the hammer site.

Just one problem: finding it in the dark.

Even leaning on the cairn – which she was

almost certain was the right one – she wasn't sure which way she'd been facing when she found the hammer. It'd help if she could see the outlines of the mountains around her, but it was way too dark for that now, and her headlamp beam definitely didn't go that far.

If only all the bloody rocks didn't look the same…

Well, they hadn't earlier, but the sun had been out then, whereas now…

She had a crazy thought. Tried to dismiss it, but it wouldn't go away. Well, if nothing else worked…

Everyone else had called the weapon Thor's hammer. The Vikings had believed in him, invoked him at every turn and wore amulets with his hammer on them. If anyone could help her…

"Thor? If you even exist, I could really use your help right now. Help finding the place where I found what everyone's calling your hammer." Oh, this was stupid. The Norse gods didn't exist. They never had. "Help.

Thor, please help me."

Something moved behind her, like a stone kicked loose by a clumsy foot, clattering against its fellows until it found a new place to settle.

Sibyl spun around, lighting up the area with the beam of her torch. Nothing. No one.

Except…wait, was that something moving?

Sibyl crept closer. At first glance, she thought it was a huntsman spider, a really big one, like they got back home. Big and pale and scary, they could be as big as your hand, but weren't actually dangerous, unless you were a bug. Or maybe a small bird or lizard.

Only…that didn't look like a spider. It didn't move like one, and it didn't have enough legs. It almost looked like…

Sibyl jumped back. That was a human hand, feeling around the rocks like it was looking for something. A hand sticking up out of the rocks like Thing from the Addams Family.

Not…possible. Hands didn't come out of graves in real life. Only in zombie movies.

Sibyl refused to watch zombie movies, because she was pretty sure they mostly ended the same way – with people being chased and killed and eaten. Nope. No way was she doing zombies.

She backed away slowly, hoping the hand wouldn't hear her and come after her. Or that the hand's owner wouldn't, if zombies could…

She almost burst out laughing. Zombies didn't exist. This had to be a prank, a joke, a battery operated toy that someone had put here to scare her. All she had to do was lean in, pick it up, and turn it off.

She took a step forward, then another. There was a slight dip in the ground level here, like the hand was in the spot where they'd found the hammer. Well, that would make sense, if someone wanted to prank her.

Sibyl stepped down, then marched forward, determined to grab the thing so she could confront the prankster and…

She'd forgotten about the ice. The layer of ice that had stopped her digging any further, that was so slick under her slippers she couldn't help but slip, unable to stop herself as she flew forward toward the cairn.

HELP, was her last desperate thought before her head connected with the cairn and darkness claimed her.

TWELVE

HELP.

The call came again, more urgent than before.

Thor knew he needed his hammer — weaponless, he'd be no match for the wolf — but the call was so insistent, he could not bear to make her wait any longer.

He rose, sliding through ice and rock as effortlessly as if it was air.

Only to discover he'd arrived too late. The lady he'd been summoned to protect lay lifeless on the rocks.

No, wait – she still drew breath. Yes, her heart still beat, for blood leaked sluggishly from a cut somewhere beneath her hair.

"I am here to protect you, mistress, as I promised," he said, lifting her in his arms.

Even though he called her mistress, knowing it was her voice that had summoned him to her side to assist her, he'd never seen this woman before in his life. Her small stature, her dark hair…surely he'd remember such things, even without a face as lovely as hers, clearly illuminated by the glowing diadem she wore.

He'd never seen anything like that, either. Crowns were fashioned in silver or gold, with gemstones, or so he'd heard. One that glowed like a star, with only light, but no heat…was wondrous. Magical, even. The only other time he'd heard of a star coming to earth had been when his father told the tale of how his hammer had been forged, from the metal of that fallen star. But the dying star his father had caught was nothing to this glimmering miracle.

His mistress must be a powerful witch to possess such magic.

But she was not dressed for snow – she did not even wear a cloak. She must not be far from camp.

Thor scanned the area. Sure enough, he could see the lights and hulking shadows of a temporary camp further down the hill, beside the lake.

All the tents were occupied but one – one that held two pallets, presumably for his mistress and her servant.

In the absence of the servant, Thor was all she had, so he tore a strip of linen from his shirt and used it to bandage her head, so that the blood would not stain her pillow.

For a long moment, he watched her sleep, wishing he dared to wake her.

Then he heard the crunch of footsteps

outside the tent.

Ah, this must be her servant. A tall, blonde girl, of an age with his mistress, but more like his own people than this little witch.

Thor knew neither woman would want him present while the servant prepared her mistress for bed, and slipped out of the tent, waiting until the servant was inside before placing himself outside the entrance to stand guard.

"None shall harm you while you sleep, mistress. I am your protector, as promised," he said, hoping she heard him. And there he remained, ever watchful.

THIRTEEN

Strong arms lifted her up, so warm she could feel the heat of him even through her snow gear as he cradled her against his chest. She heard the rumble of his voice as he said something to her that she didn't quite catch. She could only make out one word – protector. It was enough to make her smile. She was definitely dreaming now. She shouldn't have been reading romance novels before bed, because when they inspired dreams like this one, she didn't want to wake up, even when she knew it was a dream.

"Sibyl! Sibyl!"

Sibyl clenched her eyes shut against the bright light Jorunn was shining right on her face. "Unless your name is Thor and you have more muscles than a Hemsworth, all the better to carry me away to your castle in the sky, go away."

Jorunn, being her usual insouciant self, just laughed. "You can go back to dreaming about hot Vikings as soon as you tell me where and how you got that."

"Got what?" Sibyl grumbled, sitting up. That had been a mistake. Her hangover should have been gone, but now her head throbbed worse than this morning.

"And that!" Jorunn said, pointing at Sibyl's hurting head.

"Jorunn…" Sibyl began. "I have no idea what you're talking about."

"Well, first, that epic wool blanket that I've

never seen before, which you couldn't possibly have carried in your backpack here. And then there's the bloodstained bandage wrapped around your head. Even if you have been fighting Vikings in your dreams, it still doesn't explain that."

One hand went to her head, while the other stretched out to stroke the blanket. Which wasn't a blanket at all, but a cloak, for it tapered at the top, where it was attached to some sort of hood. It looked like something a hard-core reenactor would wear at one of the medieval fairs back home.

Or a Viking warrior, a thousand years ago, her traitorous mind whispered.

Jorunn tugged at the bandage and dropped it in Sibyl's lap. "I suppose you're going to tell me that's not your blood, but someone else's."

Sibyl winced as she touched the part of her head that hurt most. Dark, clotted blood clung to her fingers. "No, I think it's mine. I slipped and hit my head earlier when I…when I went to the bathroom," she lied. She did remember hitting her head. She just didn't remember getting back to her tent.

Unless she hadn't dreamed being carried…

"And I suppose Thor himself materialised, carried you back here, and gave you his cloak as a souvenir so you'd know he was real?" Jorunn asked, almost as if she could read Sibyl's mind.

"I don't remember," Sibyl said honestly. Because a dream was just that – a dream. There couldn't possibly have been a real Viking protector who'd carried her all the way back from the cairn to her tent. How had he even known it was her tent?

This had to be a prank. Whoever had planted the Addams Family hand had brought her back here, and covered her in the cloak, which had come here in one of the packhorses' panniers. There was no other possible explanation.

Sibyl climbed out of bed. She was still wearing her winter coat. Not even when she was drunk had she ever gone to bed wearing that. Someone else had definitely put her to bed, and she was going to raise hell when she found out who.

It couldn't be Nik, who must have been born without a sense of humour, and Lara and Karl were too busy managing and leading the expedition, respectively, to have time for pranking anyone. It must be one of the other expeditioners she didn't know. Well, she knew their names were Lars, Andreas and Fredrik, but she didn't know one from the other, they all looked so alike.

Just because they were tall and blonde didn't mean they had the right to manhandle her, especially when she was unconscious. If she ever found out who'd done this, she was going to ask Callie for a curse to make all his golden hair fall out.

Whoever he was, he was probably standing outside, pissing himself laughing.

Well, she was done being some idiot's laughingstock. Sibyl bundled the cloak up in her arms. "I'm going to the bathroom," she announced with as much dignity as she could muster.

"Don't hit your head again, then. Or I'll have to get Nik to help me carry you back here. I definitely couldn't do it myself," Jorunn said.

Which definitely ruled out Jorunn as the prankster. It had to be one of the men. But which one?

Luckily, Sibyl had lived long enough with Callie and Octavia to hold her own against a man much bigger than she was. She might not possess all of Callie's or Octavia's unique skills, but they didn't know that.

Sibyl stepped out of the tent. "Whoever owns this cloak, show yourself right now, or I'll burn it to ash," she announced, in a voice she was happy to hear didn't tremble at all.

FOURTEEN

Thor could not disobey a direct order, issued with such authority. He dropped to one knee before her. "You appeared cold, mistress, and you had no cloak of your own, so I covered you with mine. I realise it is not fine enough for a lady like yourself, but it was all I had, and I am sworn to protect you in all things, even from something as mundane as the cold air."

He could feel her stare boring into the top

of his head. Did he dare look up? If she intended to strike him down, it was better to see the blow coming than to wait for it in ignorance. Then at least he might look upon her face in all its beauty and…

"You can't be real. You can't be," she said, dropping the cloak on the stones at his feet.

"I assure you, mistress, I am Thor, your sworn protector, and both I and all I possess are at your service." He sucked in a breath. "Please, wear my cloak to keep you warm, until I can provide you with one that is far finer and more fitting for your station."

"I don't need a cloak. I need…"

An eternity he waited, or so it felt, but still she did not tell him what she wished for.

Finally, she said, "You can't be Thor. You don't have a hammer."

Thor hung his head. Of course she'd noticed. No wonder she had no commands for him. Without a weapon, he was hardly any protector at all. "I seem to have mislaid it," he admitted. Not entirely the truth, but he did not dare tell her that Jarl Erik and his pet wolf had taken his hammer from him. He could have sworn that Astrid had returned it to him, but that must have been a dream, for it was nowhere to be found now. "I will find a suitable weapon before sunset on the morrow, so that I might better protect you."

She huffed out an impatient breath, as if this did not meet with her satisfaction, either.

"I will protect you, mistress. I swear it, from now until my last breath," he said. "If you could persuade the other witch to return my hammer, I would use it solely in your service."

FIFTEEN

Thor? The other witch? A cloak, and now a hammer? Whoever this man was, he definitely wasn't Andreas or Lars or…Frederik, that's what the other guy's name was. She'd definitely have noticed if any of the other expeditioners had muscles like this guy, even if they didn't usually go around bare armed like he was now. Which was crazy, as it had be below freezing outside right now. Even the man's shirt hung open, so she could see his bare chest and abs and fuck he was hot…

Sibyl shook her head, which hurt, so she stopped. This guy couldn't be real. He had to be a hallucination, a product of her head injury and Lara's comments about Thor's hammer earlier, combined with too much reading and her own wild imagination.

A sensible person would ignore the Norse god kneeling at her feet, go to the bathroom tent, and then go back to bed and forget any of this had happened. If she hadn't imagined it all, in which case she should definitely forget about it.

But Sibyl had never really been that sensible. That's what had brought her halfway around the world to this alien snowscape, the complete opposite of home. So if she really was hallucinating a Norse god kneeling at her feet, then she was damn well going to see if her imagination would stretch to showing her the Norse god in all his glory, holding his hammer, before she came to her senses.

Octavia would have told her to go for it, if only so she could ask for all the details later. Alethea would tell her that even if he was a hallucination, she had to help him, because it was the right thing to do.

And she had found Thor's hammer today, hadn't she? She definitely hadn't imagined that.

Sibyl took a deep breath. Keeping her voice low, barely above a whisper, so no one else would hear her, she said, "Come with me. I might have a suitable weapon for you."

Then she forced herself to walk toward the mess tent, home to the dripping hammer that would hopefully yield enough information for her entire PhD thesis.

Her headlamp beam cut a clear path through the frosty air. Part of her mind told her she should be afraid, walking out here alone in the pitch darkness. She'd been warned about all sorts of creatures – including bears! Real, live bears! – that were found in the Jotunheimen National Park, but the clear crunch of Thor's footsteps behind her was so reassuring, she didn't fear anything right now.

Which was stupid, because even if she thought she could hear his footsteps, he wasn't really there, let alone capable of defending her against a bear or whatever else might be out there in the darkness.

Sibyl shook her head at her own silliness as she unzipped the door to the mess tent.

She swept the beam of her headlamp around the dark interior, wondering what she'd say or do if someone was still up. Not that anyone else would be able to see Thor, so it wouldn't have mattered, but…

Wordlessly, she held the door open, so he could duck inside.

The space felt so much smaller with him inside. Maybe it was partly because he was so bloody big – twice as wide as she was, even without the cloak now draped from his shoulders, and tall enough that his head brushed the ceiling. Then again, it would take a man this big to heft that hammer by himself. None of the expeditioners had been able to lift it alone, though the weight of the ice still encrusting it hadn't helped.

It was strangely silent in the tent. Just the sound of her rapid breath – nothing from Thor – without even the steady drip drip drip of the ice melting from the hammer that had punctuated the meal prep this evening.

Which meant all the ice was gone, and she'd be the first to see the hammer in all its naked glory.

She glanced behind her. Actually, she'd like to see Thor wielding his hammer, with both of them all naked and glorious, but her imagination refused to cooperate. The pants and boots and cloak stayed firmly where they were, and while his shirt still hung open, giving her plenty of to-die-for abs to ogle, he had no bare skin below the waist.

It was the hammer she should be looking at, she scolded herself. The very real hammer that definitely did exist, as opposed to the sexy man who most certainly did not.

She stepped up to the table, where they'd

left the tray with the melting hammer inside, propped up on a bunch of rocks so it wasn't sitting in a puddle of its own meltwater.

She closed her eyes. This was what she'd come here for. An artefact that could make her entire career, and she'd been lucky enough to be the one who found it. "Here it is. Thor's hammer," she breathed, opening her eyes.

Only to see nothing but a tray of wet rocks, sitting in a puddle of water.

"What the actual fuck?"

SIXTEEN

She muttered many words Thor did not understand, interspersed with ones he did. Something about how someone must have catalogued the artefact before storing it properly, and she'd ask about it in the morning. She also said FUCK a lot, a word he thought he understood, but she did not appear the slightest bit interested in engaging in such an activity, so he decided to ask her about it later, when she did not appear so angry.

What he did gather was that there was a weapon she'd had in mind for him to wield, and it was not where she expected it to be.

No matter. While he would gladly accept whatever magical weapon she might provide, there were others buried in the ice that might serve. He would spend the day searching, and when night fell on the morrow, he would be properly armed to defend her.

She stormed back to her own tent, and Thor chose wisely to stay outside. An angry witch could curse him in ways he could not even imagine, and he would be a poor protector indeed if he provoked her ire so much that she turned him into a worm or a toad or some other lowly creature.

He waited until both she and her servant were asleep, before daring to venture away from her tent in search of a weapon. There had to be something buried in the ice he might use.

Thor had not taken three steps from the

camp before he spotted a shadow moving down near the lake. There was something familiar about the way it moved…

In an instant, he was running along the lakeshore, tackling the shadow to the ground. "You stole my hammer! I know it was you! Return it at once!"

Loki struggled beneath him, but he could not throw Thor off. "I haven't touched your hammer. That thing's too big to be of use to anyone. Why you don't use an axe like a normal warrior…"

Thor shoved Loki deeper into the sand. "That was my father's weapon, made from a dying star. I've killed more men with it in a day than you have in your entire life. Just because you are too weak to lift it…tell me where you have hidden it, so we can both protect our new mistress together, as brothers in arms once more."

Loki turned his head and spat on the ground. "I would rather die than serve that witch. I'm no traitor. I only wish I had taken your hammer, so that I might use it to knock some sense into you. We are Odin's men, not Erik's, no matter what spell that witch cast. You shouldn't be protecting her, you should be killing her, along with Erik and all his men."

"No. Our mistress is not Erik's daughter, but a different witch. One far more powerful. She had a crown with a living star that glows. We must protect her," Thor insisted.

"You sound like a fool. You do mean the girl who slipped on the ice, without the wit to wear proper boots or even a cloak against the cold? Whatever she's done to make you think she has power, you're wrong. It's a trick, I tell you, and the sooner you see through it, the sooner you will be free of her influence, as I am. You don't see me carrying her about the place, or standing outside in the cold outside her tent!"

Of course Loki had seen everything. He was their sneakiest scout, creeping about unseen. How he'd managed to miss Erik's men lying in wait for them on the plain below the pass,

Thor still couldn't fathom.

But this argument wasn't about the past, but the present. And protecting the witch.

"If you seek to harm her, I will not allow it. Though you are my brother in arms, and the closest thing I have to a blood brother, I will cut you down where you stand before you can lay a hand on her," Thor warned him.

Loki sighed loudly. "Fine. You are under the witch's spell. You'll feel like even more of a fool when I find out how to break it. You always did have a soft spot for pretty women. Teaching your sister to fight was the most foolish thing you ever did, until today."

"Sif is now feasting in Valhalla, the best any warrior could hope for. Say one more word about Sif and it will be the last thing you ever say," Thor growled.

Loki rolled his eyes. "So now your sister is a better warrior than both of us put together. Happy now?"

Put like that, Thor could not help but laugh. "You might be right. She would be pleased to hear you say that." Grudgingly, he released his grip on Loki.

Loki clambered to his feet, shook out his cloak and dusted off his tunic. "So what are you going to do now?"

"You're going to help me search for a suitable weapon that I can use until I find my hammer again. Once I have that, I'm going to go back to watching over the witch, as I swore I would," Thor said smugly. "Then you may do as you wish."

"I can promise you I won't be serving some strange woman, no matter how pretty she is," Loki muttered.

Thor could only laugh. One day, Loki might meet a woman who would make him want to change all his ways. Until then, he could complain about them all he wanted. It was only a matter of time.

SEVENTEEN

When Sibyl awoke the next morning, she had a pounding headache and blood on her pillow to tell her last night definitely hadn't been a dream. Well, except for Thor, that is, who was nowhere to be seen.

Nor was Jorunn, who'd already made her bed and headed out for the day.

Sibyl struggled into a fresh set of thermals and her outer gear, before heading out to join the rest of the team.

"Is it true?" Lara greeted her as Sibyl entered the mess tent.

That she'd had a hallucination so hot, she'd even dreamed about him? No way was Sibyl admitting to that. They'd all think she was crazy.

"Is what true?" Sibyl asked wearily, heading straight for the coffee pot. She needed two cups before she'd be good for anything today.

"That you tripped and fell on the way to the bathroom last night, hit your head and don't remember how you got back to your tent," Jorunn said. She stared studiously at the ground. "I told them. I was worried about you. Especially when I couldn't wake you up this morning."

Maybe hitting her head explained the hallucinations, too. Well, just one hallucination. His Norse Hotness.

Sibyl sighed. "Yes. I think there's blood in my hair, and I'd give my eyeteeth for a proper shower right now."

Karl bustled in. "Well, with a possible concussion, safety procedures say you might just get that shower sooner than you think. When Jakop arrives with the packhorses tomorrow, you'll be headed back to civilisation with him, and you're not to come back until you get the all clear from a doctor. Safety first."

Sibyl put down her coffee cup. "I can't just leave! This is my PhD project. I have to keep working. We need to revisit the site where we found the hammer and see what else might be there."

"As I told you last night, with snow forecast for this morning, and a cold snap forecast after that, it won't be practical to investigate that site for some months, until more of the ice has melted. Plenty of time for you to go back to town, get checked out, and return." Karl shook his head. "You're not allowed back at work until I see a doctor's certificate declaring you fit for work."

Jorunn poured herself a cup of coffee. "I

don't know what you're complaining about. A couple days off, then a nice horse ride over the mountains back to town, where you'll have a hot shower, heating and a real bed, plus the whole lab facility to yourself, alone with Thor's hammer, where you'll be able to run every test you can think of. If the news crews get a hold of the story, you might even hit the news in Australia. That hammer is a significant find all on its own, and the news cameras will lap it up, it's so shiny and all."

Sibyl's eyes darted to the tray where the hammer had been last night. It was still gone. "Wait, the hammer's going back to town, too?"

Lara nodded. "Nik did all the paperwork and packed it up for you last night. He must really like you, to have done all that. All our finds to date are being sent back to the lab for safekeeping. One of the perks of having a regular supply run. The donkeys come here with full packs, but there's plenty of space to take whatever we need back to town with them. This is better for everyone."

Sibyl was torn. On the one hand, she wanted to be here, where she just knew there was more to find. On the other hand, if she could just x-ray the hammer, and use the internet connection in town to research what other non-destructive testing she could do on it, plus get something to stop her head from feeling like she'd been on the biggest bender ever…maybe it wouldn't be so bad.

"Can you pick up some chocolate while you're in town? I'm nearly out and there's no way I'll make it through the rest of the season without chocolate," Jorunn wheedled.

An entire archaeological dig without chocolate? Even Sibyl didn't want to imagine that. "Sure. I guess I'll have nothing better to do while I'm there," she said. She should probably pick up some more chocolate for herself, too, while she was at it.

EIGHTEEN

Whatever the witch Astrid had done to him, Thor could no longer tolerate sunlight, so it was with great reluctance that Thor was forced to take refuge in the icy rocks beneath her tent, instead of standing tall outside of it. That didn't mean his watch had ended. No, the spell the witch had cast had banished his need for sleep and even sustenance, allowing him to remain on guard for as long as his new mistress needed him.

She no longer wore her glowing star crown in daylight, and even when the snow started to fall, she did not wear a cloak. Instead, she fastened a sort of short hooded tunic around her, and pulled the hood up to cover her hair. Thor longed to offer her his own heavy cloak again, but he didn't dare venture into the sunlight.

At least he had the reassurance of knowing she was not cold, despite her strange choice of dress.

He paid little attention to the sturdy donkeys when they arrived or as they were unloaded, but when they made preparations to depart and his mistress climbed upon the back of one, Thor could focus on nothing else.

She was leaving?

What did she expect him to do, with her gone?

He slipped through ice and rock, until he lay directly beneath his mistress's mount.

"What are your orders, mistress?" he

whispered, so none but she could hear him.

Her and the skittish creature she sat upon, as the donkey shied and danced about, threatening to unseat her.

She was so busy trying to stay on the donkey's back, she did not reply, and Thor was forced to watch, helpless to assist her, as she calmed the creature. Thor couldn't help but admire her skill. He preferred goats to horses — it took far more to spook a goat, and a spooked goat was more likely to headbutt whatever had startled it, instead of bolting.

He dared not speak to her again while her mount was near, which gave him his answer: he must watch over her as closely as he dared, which meant following her to her destination, as best he could.

Luckily, the ground was frozen for miles in every direction, a mix of ice and rock that permitted him to slide through it like a hot knife through butter. He would follow the witch and hope that by journey's end, he had earned her trust enough to learn her name.

But first, he needed to find a weapon, in case he needed to defend her…

Oh, but the donkeys were leaving.

No matter. He would find something along the way, he was sure of it. There were more secrets hidden under the ice than even he knew, even with the curious abilities the curse had granted him.

But was it truly a curse, if it placed him under the command of such an enchanting witch? There were worse mistresses, and masters, he could be serving right now…

The donkeys moved, and Thor followed.

NINETEEN

The higher they rose in altitude, the sharper the wind became, knifing through Sibyl's outer layers and all the way through to the other side. Maybe if she dismounted and walked beside the horse, she'd have been warmer, but Karl had given her strict orders to take it easy, just in case, and he'd made sure Jakop, the owner of the packhorses, would remind her if she forgot.

So she stayed on the animal, feeling like an ever increasing lump of ice, until Jakop called a halt for the night.

"We'll camp here. I have a spare tent in this bag for you," Jakop said, pulling out a pair of swags from the pannier of the horse in front of Sibyl's. She dismounted clumsily and probably would have dropped the swag if she hadn't tangled her numb fingers in the drawstring closure of the swag's outer covering.

Luckily, the swag was pretty much the same as the ones she'd used on expeditions back home, so it didn't need much thought to set up. When it was done, it was basically a big canvas sarcophagus – long and wide and tall enough for a human body wrapped in a big sleeping bag to lie down in, and not much else.

The problem was…it was almost exactly like the ones at home, and while those were fine for a winter's night in the Australian desert, they did bugger all against an icy wind sent straight from the North Pole.

After half an hour in her sleeping bag, when

her shivering had grown so bad, she was scared she'd bite through her own tongue, her teeth were chattering so hard, she began to wonder if it was safe to go to sleep at all. That was how people died of hypothermia, wasn't it? They went to sleep and just didn't wake up?

What she'd give for the little Everest-rated dome tent she shared with Jorunn back at camp. Or even just Jorunn, because having a roommate would have helped immeasurably.

She thought of last night's hallucination. Having His Norse Hotness in her tent or even in her sleeping bag right now, for real, would be even better.

Something crunched on the rocks outside her tent.

A bear? A wolverine? One of the reindeer Jorunn kept talking about?

Maybe it was just Jakop or one of the horses, doing their business before going to bed.

Except…she could feel the presence out there. It wasn't going away, even if it was standing still.

"Go away!" she hissed.

Whatever it was shifted, but still it didn't leave.

"But you summoned me, mistress. Do you no longer need my help?"

That was Thor, all right, or at least the voice she'd imagined belonged to the dream-Thor she'd conjured up.

This was crazy, Sibyl knew, but so was freezing to death. She'd try anything once.

She unzipped her tent. "Quick, come in here and warm me up," she said, before her courage failed her.

TWENTY

Thor hesitated. His mistress wasn't the first woman to invite him into her bed – nor the second or the third – but surely he was supposed to be protecting her, not seducing her. Yet if that was what she wanted, he'd willingly bed her. Every night, if that was her desire.

"Come on, it's freezing, and you're letting the cold air in," she snapped.

Thor hurried to obey, sliding into the low tent beside her as her shaking fingers worked at the fastenings to close the entrance again. He wrapped his hand around hers to help her, only to find her hands were as cold as the snow outside.

"Let me do that, mistress," he begged, tugging at the fastening, as he'd seen her do. By some magic, the tent sealed itself as his hand passed over it.

"S-s-s-Sibyl," she said. "My name is Sibyl. Stop calling me mistress. You're my hallucination and I summoned you, and I want you to use my name."

Thor ducked his head, for he could not kneel in obeisance in the close confines of her tent. "Yes, Miss Sibyl."

Now he was this close to her, he could not help but notice how violently her body shivered. "You should have kept my cloak, Miss Sibyl, and worn it while you were riding. Now you are too cold, and I fear for your life if we do not get you warmed up."

"That's…what you're…here for," she managed to say through chattering teeth.

Yes. He was her protector. The cold air could kill as surely as any blade, as he well knew. He should have protected her better on the journey.

He should have found something better for her bed than the thin silks she currently shivered beneath. She needed furs, or at least fine wool. The best he could offer her was his cloak, so he unfastened it and spread it over her. Better, but still not enough.

Her sleeping silks had a fastening similar to the one at the entrance to the tent. Thor hooked a finger through the loop and dragged it downward, so the silks parted at the seam. Inside, she wore underthings that were not much thicker than the silks. Underthings that covered her body even as they clung to it, leaving little to the imagination.

He wanted to stare, to drink in her beauty, but he did not dare. Not yet.

Instead, he climbed inside the silks beside

her, and tugged the magical fastener back into place.

"What are you doing? There isn't room for two of us in my sleeping bag!" she protested.

Sadly, she was right – no amount of magic would stretch the fabric around his broad shoulders, but it didn't need to, as long as he put his body between hers and the cold.

Now to warm her in earnest.

Thor took a deep breath, leaned forward, and pressed his lips to hers.

TWENTY-ONE

The sensible part of Sibyl's head said there was no way His Norse Hotness would fit in her sleeping bag, but as he crowded in beside her, she had to admit that maybe it was possible. He was her hallucination, after all, and if she was going to freeze to death tonight, then spending her final moments pressed up against the hard body of a man who'd make even a Hemsworth green with envy seemed like a pretty good way to go.

So when his surprisingly warm lips touched hers, she surrendered to what had to be a dream. Because no real, human man could possibly kiss like that. Gentle at first, but insistent, as her lips moulded to, then moved with his. He tasted of glacier ice and ozone, every bit the Norse God of Thunder, but the scent of woodsmoke clung to him, too, as though he'd just stepped out of a Viking longhouse, to appear a thousand years into the future in her bed, cold as it was.

Not so cold now.

One huge hand cupped her cheek, as the other stroked her hair, his burning touch igniting fire trails deep within her.

Down and down and down, his hands stroked, coaxing life back into her numb fingers as his hands engulfed hers.

With every stroke of his hands, he awoke more of her, riding out the pins and needles that turned to painful tingles before she was almost purring like a cat. And, just like any self-satisfied cat, she wanted more.

Her thermal shirt rode up a little, baring her tummy to his touch. The sear of his skin against hers felt almost electric. She wouldn't have been surprised to see a shower of sparks in the darkness. If he'd only slide his hand up a little further and cup her breast.

But he had other ideas, his fingers questing lower.

"Yes, Thor, please," she breathed, hardly daring to hope.

But he was her hallucination, wasn't he?

Hot, calloused fingers crept beneath her waistband, unerringly seeking her aching core. His first stroke across her clit set all her nerve endings alight.

"Yessss…"

He'd taken her from numbing cold to feeling everything, trembling from the sheer sensation of his hands on her, and she wanted more.

She reached for his belt, determined to free him, as her first orgasm hit. More powerful than any lightning strike, he left her stunned, barely able to breathe or even see, even as she felt a second one building. The second swept her away, leaving her gasping, hot on the heels of an impossible third one, bigger and better than anything she'd ever felt before. Before…before…

She came to, half sobbing, with her face pressed against his rock hard chest. She wasn't sure whether to beg for more, or if her body would explode if he touched her again.

"Sleep, Sibyl, my sweet mistress. I shall keep you warm until dawn, with my cloak wrapped around us both. I will protect you for as long as you desire," he whispered, pressing his lips to her forehead.

Always and forever, she thought, but didn't say, as she drifted into blissful sleep.

TWENTY-TWO

Sibyl packed her swag up with ruthless efficiency in the morning. Thor, with his magic hands and warm cloak, had disappeared before the first rays of dawn filtered through the fabric of her tent, and Jakop wasn't acting any differently, so he likely hadn't heard her and Thor last night.

Well, just her, really, seeing as he was a figment of her overactive imagination. When meant what had happened could only be called masturbation, she told herself. Something any healthy woman did in the absence of a suitable partner to help her. And if that partner was her imaginary friend…

God, she needed to get her head checked out. Good thing she was headed for civilisation. If she'd imagined a night like last night while sharing a tent with Jorunn, she wouldn't have known where to look this morning. Not to mention Jorunn would likely have teased her mercilessly, before asking for details about her hot dream guy.

"How long until we reach town?" Sibyl asked Jakop, as he strapped her swag back onto a packhorse.

"If the worst of the weather has blown over, and the snow stays on the other side of the mountains, we should have you back at the university labs before sundown," Jakop said.

Sibyl breathed a sigh of relief. "So we won't be freezing our butts off in tents again tonight?"

Jakop frowned. "If you were cold, you should have said something. I have extra blankets in one of the saddlebags."

Now he told her. "I was fine," she said.

He nodded. "There's enough hot water for one more cup of coffee, if you want it before we go."

Even if she was crazy, she wasn't silly enough to turn down a hot drink, so Sibyl downed her coffee while Jakop finished loading the horses.

Today her head wasn't anywhere near as painful as yesterday, and she even managed to dismount and walk some of the way beside her horse, as the narrow track widened enough to allow it.

They'd left the bone-chilling wind on the other side of the mountain, so the final leg back to the lab seemed almost balmy compared to yesterday. Sibyl began to wonder if she'd dreamed the cold, too.

When they arrived at the university's converted warehouse that doubled as both laboratory and accommodation facilities, Sibyl helped Jakop carry the boxes of artefacts into the lab. It was too early in the season for the lab manager to be in residence – she spent most of the academic year at the main university campus, and only came up here later in the summer, Lara had said – so Sibyl would be the sole university staff member here. That meant not having to share any of the lab equipment, plus having her pick of the rooms, instead of being stuck in the overflow bunkroom like she had when she'd first arrived.

Food wouldn't be a problem, either, Lara had told her. The cafeteria had a massive walk in fridge and freezer, full of frozen meals in case the team had to evacuate because of bad weather. Jorunn had teased her that she'd better get used to eating pickled herring, just like the Vikings, because that's what most of the supplies were, but a quick peek in the freezer told Sibyl that while the fridge might have a plentiful supply of fish, the freezer had a much wider selection. Sibyl had her eye on a frozen pizza, if she could work out how to turn the oven on in the adjoining ultra-modern kitchen.

Maybe she should have worked a few more shifts in Tacey's café back home – then she'd know how to use all that equipment. Then again, Tacey's oven had been bought from a decommissioned bakery, and it showed, while this thing wouldn't have looked out of place on the International Space Station.

"I'll just finish unloading, and then I'll take the donkeys home. They've earned a stay in the stable. I'll call you when we head back up the mountain, so you can return with us," Jakop said.

Reluctantly, Sibyl put the pizza back in the freezer. "I should help with that." She followed Jakop outside, to where he was already leading the horses…no, wait, he'd said they were donkeys…to an outbuilding on the edge of the compound.

He undid the straps on a plastic barrel and

carefully carried it into the shed.

"What's in those, and why aren't they going into the lab with everything else?" Sibyl asked.

"These are the refuse capsules, and you don't want them in your nice, clean laboratory. When we have a full truckload, I call the waste facility to come and pick them up. You'll want them well away from the main building, in case any of them leaks."

Sibyl stared at the barrels Jakop was rapidly lining up along the wall. "And by refuse, you mean…?"

"Any waste from the expedition. You're camping in a national park, and the rules are that you must carry all waste out with you. Food scraps and packaging from the kitchen, empty bottles, plus the tanks from the bathroom."

Sibyl backed away. "Which ones are the toilet tanks?" Not that she wanted to get near any of them, but…

Jakop laughed. "The heavy ones that I'm handling with the most care. Don't worry.

They froze solid before I loaded them, and they're still mostly frozen. It's not until we get some really warm weather and it all starts to melt that you might have a problem. Or I will, for you'll be back in the camp, digging up history, before you know it."

She sure hoped so.

"Anyway, I won't take any more of your time. See you in a week or two, when I'm due to do another supply run. Call me if you need anything," he said.

She waved goodbye and headed back inside. Pizza was calling, followed by Thor's hammer.

TWENTY-THREE

Sibyl set her laptop up on a table in the cafeteria, and was deep in a journal database search for suitable tests to perform on medieval weapons when the timer for the pizza went off.

Most of the non-destructive testing involved x-ray imaging of some sort or another, though for some of the more detailed tests, she'd need specialist equipment only found in a large hospital or industrial testing facility. Something to ask Karl or the laboratory manager about when they were all in the lab together again, Sibyl decided.

She'd also managed to book a doctor's appointment at the local medical centre, but as the earliest they'd had available was still several days away, she didn't need to worry about that yet.

She reached for another slice of pizza, only to realise she'd polished off the whole plate. Huh. She couldn't remember the last time she'd eaten a whole pizza. Back home, she'd always had a few slices leftover for breakfast the next day.

Unless Octavia found them first, while working through the night on some super secret project, which was what she was likely to be doing at this very moment, while the other residents of Bell House slept.

Sibyl should probably get some sleep, too. Shower, then sleep.

"This has to be the biggest hall I have ever

seen. I've heard tales of kings, far in the west, who have such huge halls, but never had I seen one with my own eyes until today. Which king rules here?"

For the first time, she got a good look at His Norse Hotness, and had to admit, he was even hotter than she remembered.

Long, blonde hair hung to his shoulders, over which was draped the cloak he'd laid over her last night. Right before he'd used nothing more than his fingers to give her the three best orgasms of her life. In the light of her headlamp, she'd thought the cloak was black, but the wool was in fact a deep blue, trimmed with cream fur. His shirt hung open, baring his sculpted chest and abs, which ended in a sort of short kilt in the same blue, fastened around his narrow waist with a thick leather belt that looked like something a wrestler had won. Leather boots covered his well-muscled calves almost to the knee.

And in his hand he held a thick staff, topped by…

"Is that a poleaxe?" It was taller than she was, and more of a medieval weapon than a Viking one. "Where did you get that?"

He shrugged his massive shoulders. "I found it under the ice. It had a frozen skull spiked to the top of it, which I had to shake off, before cleaning it, for I did not think you would want your protector standing beside you with a bloodstained axe. It seemed a suitable weapon, until I find my hammer. The handle is unusually long, a bit unwieldy, so I thought I might cut it down to a better size, if you could provide me with a suitable axe." He looked expectantly at her.

Hallucination or not, no way was she going to stand by and allow him to destroy valuable artefacts. "A poleaxe is a perfectly adequate weapon for any fighter. There are plenty of manuals that have survived from medieval times, explaining polearm fighting techniques. In fact, I remember watching an online video not long ago..." She typed in a search on her laptop and two videos popped up at the top of the first page. She started to turn her laptop around to show him, then remembered he was only a hallucination, and shook her head. "What you're going to do is put that back where you found it, along with the skull and whatever else was with it, and I'll show you where your hammer is, okay?"

"Very well, Miss Sibyl." Then he just stood there, looking expectant.

Well, she had intended to take a look at the artefacts after dinner. Now was as good a time as any.

So she rose, leaving her laptop and dirty dishes behind, and headed to the lab.

TWENTY-FOUR

"I don't believe it! It's not here!"

Sibyl's anger simmered in the air. Thor wished he could punch whichever man or men were the source of it, but there was no one in this enormous building but the two of them.

"I'll check again, in case I missed something," she said.

Once more, she methodically opened each of the boxes, examining the contents, before closing each one and moving onto the next.

Thor spotted a number of arrows, some familiar and some very crude, a shoe, several pieces of bedraggled cloth, a bunch of bones that looked like they'd once belonged to a horse or three, and…

"A reindeer training harness. I haven't seen one of these in years. Not since we ran out of fodder one long, cold winter, so we had to slaughter everything but the goats. The ground was still frozen when we should have been ploughing and planting, so I announced that I'd train the goats to pull the plough. Everyone laughed, thinking it a great jest, but I found a reindeer training harness that fitted around their horns and hitched them up to a cart. It took time and patience and a lot of cursing – enough for some of the men to go out in search of oxen or horses or even reindeer to replace what we'd lost – but I did it. Those goats were the best matched pair I ever worked with, though they'd show anyone else their teeth if they tried to harness them," Thor shook his head fondly, as he reverently placed the pieces of wood back in their box.

He looked up to find Sibyl staring at him in wonder. "That's what they are? I can't wait to see Jorunn again so I can tell her. She is obsessed with reindeer. She keeps telling me how there are hundreds of them in the national park, but she has yet to see one."

"Which one was Jorunn?" Thor asked. He hadn't paid much attention to the other people at the camp, but if they were important to Sibyl, it was best that he learned as much as he could about them.

"We shared a tent. When she saw your cloak on my bed the night I first saw you, for a moment, I thought she was going to fight me for it. It's not reindeer hide, is it?"

Thor grinned. "No, it's fine wool. The sort of garment you should wear outside, instead of flimsy silk."

"My jacket is nylon, not silk, and it's full of duck down. It's probably not as suitable for the Arctic as something like sealskin, but until yesterday, I was doing just fine with it. I guess the windproofing just didn't hold up to polar winds, is all."

More words Thor did not understand. "If you want a sealskin cloak, I could…" he began eagerly.

"No! We don't steal artefacts, and we don't slaughter seals. For someone who's wholly the product of my damaged brain, you sure have some archaic ideas. Ideas you can't possibly have gotten from me."

"What about bear fur? It's not quite as waterproof as sealskin, but it's the warmest…"

Sibyl raised a hand to halt him. "No fur or skin or killing anything. I don't even need a coat in here, now the heating's on. See? I'm taking my coat off." As if to demonstrate, she draped the garment over the back of her chair. "I don't need anything heavier than a sweater inside now." She gestured toward the short moss-green tunic she now wore.

It looked more like fur than wool, but Thor had never known a creature to have green fur before. "What kind of creature has a pelt like this?" he asked, reaching out to stroke it.

She pulled away, out of reach. "Do you want me to find your hammer or not? Because that's what we're here for. I'm going through all the boxes just in case I missed something, but what I really want to do is take a shower. Maybe it would be better if I did that and came back to the lab in the morning to look for the hammer. It has to be here, so I must have just missed it. Or maybe Jakop put the box in a different lab, or the store room, or maybe it got mixed up with my stuff. I don't know. I'm tired and my head hurts and…is there any chance you can wait until morning for your hammer?"

When she put it like that, how could he refuse? Thor inclined his head. "Of course, Miss Sibyl. I have my poleaxe with which to defend you. You may sleep soundly, knowing I will watch over you as you sleep."

"From outside the door. No poleaxes in the bedroom, or the bathroom, okay? And no pretending to be a creepy vampire stalker, watching me while I sleep, either."

She did seem to have a great many rules, but they were not difficult to remember. "It shall be as you wish, Miss Sibyl."

She swallowed. "And about last night…"

Thor grinned. "Do you wish me to warm your bed again tonight? Outside of the confines of that tent, I can give you even greater pleasure. All night, if that is your wish."

For a moment, she looked wistful, like she was about to agree, and Thor's hopes soared.

Then she shook her head. "I think I'll be warm enough by myself tonight, thanks. Yeah. Thanks." She wandered out of the room, leaving her coat behind.

Along with Thor's dashed hopes. He'd looked too high. Last night, she'd needed his warmth, and he'd happily given it to her, but now…she had no need for him, as lover or protector or anything, really.

If only he had his hammer, and he could show her what sort of warrior he truly was.

Then perhaps she might value him, if only a little.

Thor sighed. He could wait until morning for that. Better that she be well rested and in a better mood, for then she'd be more appreciative of what he had to offer her.

At least, he hoped so, for after last night…

Was it wrong to lust after the woman he was bound to protect? For he'd been able to think of nothing and no one else, and he feared one night with her had ruined him for all other women.

Just the way she moaned his name at the peak of her pleasure…

It was a memory he would treasure all his days, he promised himself.

TWENTY-FIVE

After a shower, an amazing night's sleep in a real bed, followed by an even longer shower the next morning, Sibyl was ready for work. She carefully stored each and every artefact she and Jakop had brought in yesterday, but still she didn't find the hammer. So she went through the other labs and store rooms, checking everything. She found all sorts of things – including the x-ray machine – but

Thor's hammer had vanished as if it had never existed.

Luckily, she didn't have to break the news to him, because her hallucination had disappeared as readily as his hammer. Maybe she only saw him when she was really tired, or her head really hurt. She'd never had hallucinations before, and she hoped this would be the end of it.

Her appointment with the doctor came and went – and she left the clinic with a clean bill of health and a medical certificate she could wave at Karl to tell him she was fit for work again.

She called Jakop, who said he'd be heading back out to the expedition site in a little over a week, which gave her eight days to read some more journal articles, wash all her clothes, and enjoy luxuries like the kitchen, the shower and a real bed, while they lasted.

Her only regret was that she hadn't managed to get naked with imaginary Thor before she recovered. If you were going to hallucinate a hot Norse god, at least you should sample all the goods, so to speak. It wasn't like that loincloth he'd worn had left much to the imagination.

She'd even made a couple of trips up to the little shop in town, to stock up on alcohol and chocolate for Jorunn, as promised. On impulse, she'd bought a bottle of mead, as well. It wasn't as strong as aquavit, but she figured she'd drink as much of it as she could while she was here. It wasn't like there was anything else to do at night.

Tonight, she'd decided to take a leaf out of Tacey's book and try to cook her own dinner, instead of reheating something from the freezer. She'd found a Norwegian recipe for something that resembled tuna mornay, if you made it with cod instead of tuna, and the name roughly translated to fish gratin, so she figured she could manage it. Even better, the store had been able to provide all the ingredients, including the breadcrumbs and cheese to go on top.

As she served up, she wondered what Thor would have said about it. Fish was traditional Viking food, and they'd probably had some sort of cheese, but pasta wouldn't have made it onto the menu until well after the Viking age was over.

Probably a good thing, seeing as the Norse god's hard body had definitely looked like the product of a high protein diet, not one rich in carbs. Maybe the cheese, though...

"FUCK!"

While she'd been daydreaming, the cheese sauce had trickled down the spoon and onto her hand, and it felt like it was just a shade cooler than molten lava.

Sibyl raced to stick her hand under some cold, running water.

"Miss Sibyl, I hope you don't mind me asking, but...in your language, what does FUCK mean?"

Sibyl took a deep breath. That couldn't have been Thor. The doctor had said she was fine, so she couldn't possibly be hallucinating...His

Norse Hotness behind her, in the kitchen. Cloak, hard abs, poleaxe and all.

"It's a coarse term for engaging in sexual intercourse, but in the present context, it's a curse word, signifying that I burned myself and am in a lot of pain," Sibyl said. "Which you should know, if you're a figment of my imagination. I mean, you speak and understand English, despite looking like a Viking from the first millennium, before this language even existed."

Thor frowned. "I believe my familiarity with your language is part of the magic that binds me to you. As I am sworn to serve you, I must understand your commands. Most of them, I do, except for some words that do not seem to make sense in any language. Nylon, for example. I do not know this word." He peered at her plate. "And I do not recognise this food, though it does smell of fish. I believe I would like it."

Sibyl's mind was starting to connect the dots, and she wasn't sure what was crazier: that this man was a hallucination, or that he wasn't.

"You knew things about reindeer training harness. I didn't even know anyone harnessed reindeer for anything, except maybe Santa Claus in the stories. Jorunn might know that, but I certainly didn't," she said.

Thor nodded. "Oh, reindeer are surprisingly useful, and so easy to train! Much better than horses or goats, and they can live off the land, better than even we can. I mean, I trained goats to till the fields, but the other men brought back reindeer, and I have to admit, I watched with considerable envy. Sure, my seeds went into the ground sooner and I had an earlier harvest, but the next season, they had all the advantages. Mostly because Loki was driving too fast with my goats hitched up to the cart, and one tripped and broke its leg, so the cart rolled over and killed the other one, so that was the end of them, and I had to start over with a new pair. In the end, I journeyed into the mountains and captured some reindeer of my own."

Jorunn should hear this. Jorunn would want to hear this. Jorunn, who'd seen Thor's cloak that first night, when Thor must have carried her back to her tent, because there was no way she could have gotten there otherwise. She couldn't be hallucinating him, if Jorunn had seen his cloak.

Why hadn't she realised all of this earlier?

Before the night he'd climbed into her tent and pleasured her, and she'd stopped only because she knew he wasn't real…

"You're real." Sibyl said softly, turning off the tap. She dried her hands on her pants, then reached toward Thor's face. Stubble scraped her palm as she cupped his cheek. "You're Thor, and you're really here."

He frowned. "Yes, Miss Sibyl, of course I'm real. I'm your protector, as I told you. You summoned me."

He'd told her that, but she hadn't understood. "I don't know how. I mean, I can't even order a pizza here, which is why I've been eating frozen ones. Summoning a thousand-year-old Norse god…well, you've got to admit, it's hard to believe." She wasn't sure she wanted to believe it, even if she couldn't deny the evidence of her own eyes.

"A thousand years? Truly, have I slept so long?" He covered her hand with his own. "No wonder your world seems to strange to me, and the words!" A look of wonder lit his face.

And that made no sense at all. If she'd been asleep for a thousand years and been woken up by some PhD student, she'd be spitting chips. "How can you be so calm about this? Is there some Zen school all gods get to go to? Like in Percy Jackson? Or is that just for demigods?"

Now he frowned. "I do not know this Percy, son of Jack."

Laughter bubbled up. "Well, no, you wouldn't. It's a kids' book, and if you need to ask what fuck means, there's a whole lot of history and culture you'd need to catch up on."

Thor stepped closer, so that barely a breath separated them. "You are mistaken, Miss Sibyl.

I am very familiar with fucking in all its forms, and it would be my pleasure to show you." His voice was so deep, it was almost a growl. One that did wicked things to her insides.

The sensible part of her brain was screaming that this was a thousand-year-old Norse god, who could do anything he wanted to her.

Her body, and the lust-filled haze that was the rest of her brain, whispered that not only did His Norse Hotness want to do all sorts of things to her, he'd already done some of them, and she'd wanted more ever since.

"Thor?" she whispered.

"I am yours to command, Miss Sibyl. What would you have me do?"

She swallowed. Those eyes. Glowing blue like a glacier lit from within. "Me. I want you to do me."

TWENTY-SIX

His lips landed on hers, and she didn't hesitate this time. She knew this was no fever dream, and that the muscles she gripped were every bit as real as how much she ached for him. She wasn't sure how this was possible, that she'd summoned a hot Viking warrior from a previous century, but she could question that part later. Right now, the part she was most interested in was poking her in the tummy and she wanted to feel it inside her.

She wrapped her legs around his hips and climbed him like a koala. Much better, even if there were still too many clothes between them.

God, but he could kiss…

She almost didn't notice his hands cupping her butt, grinding her against him until she almost cried out at how good that felt.

She shucked off her jacket, then made short work of the clothes she could take off until she was bare to the waist. She couldn't take her pants off without climbing down, and she didn't want to let go. Never wanted to let go.

"By the gods, you're beautiful. Absolutely perfect," he murmured as he pressed his lips to one nipple, then the other. Then he started to suck, and she lost all reason.

Gasping, she peered up at him. "I didn't even know it was possible to come without you touching me down there."

"I want to touch you everywhere. To see all of you as you moan my name like you did last night. To see if you truly are as beautiful in ecstasy as I imagined."

"Yes, yes!" Anything. Everything.

She was too distracted by his kisses to realise he was moving until her back hit the wall. It might have knocked the breath out of her, if she hadn't been so breathless already. Holding her in place with one hand, he tugged her pants, then her knickers off with the other.

"You're wetter than you were last night," he marvelled.

With him between her thighs, was it any wonder? If this were a romance novel, he'd have melted her underwear right off with a look. "Please, Thor." Words she never thought she'd say outside of dreams. But this was no dream. She knew that for certain.

"Tell me what you want, Miss Sibyl. Tell me, so that I can give it to you."

She reached under his loincloth, for the bulge she could barely wrap her fingers around. Talk about huge. "I want you to make love to me, Thor. Like last night, only…more.

Much more."

"I might be too big for you, Miss Sybil. With you still a maiden…I do not want to hurt you."

Sibyl had never laughed so hard in her life. "I'm not a virgin. Last night wasn't even my first time sharing a swag with a guy. It might be a tight fit, especially with a man as big as you, but we'll make it work." It took her a moment to realise there were two ways he could take that. What did it matter? She should have done this with him last night. "I want your cock, Thor. I want you to take me right here, against this wall. Hard and fast and…god, I need to feel you inside me. Now, Thor."

He'd been big in her hands, but as the head of his cock slid between her thighs, she swore he'd grown even bigger. But as he buried himself to the hilt inside her, filling her completely as he rubbed against all the right spots, she forgot everything else except the hard molten heat of him. In her. Against her.

Pressing her against the wall, holding her up when her legs wouldn't hold her…

"Fuck me, Thor, harder," she panted.

And oh god he did.

She screamed his name, holding on for dear life as the first orgasm conquered her, stealing her breath and her heart.

"Miss Sibyl…"

"Don't stop. Please, don't stop. More, Thor, please!"

The second orgasm left her trembling, barely able to cling to him as she whimpered his name.

And the third…the third…

"Fuck! Thor!"

TWENTY-SEVEN

Sibyl trembled in his arms as he carried her to the finest bed in the building. He was still just as hard for her as he'd been in her tent last night – another of the curse's gifts – but while she begged for more, he knew she'd get cold if he kept her out in the feasting hall for too long.

Of course, once he'd laid her on the bed, he paused to let his eyes drink their fill. She might be small and delicate, but his Sibyl was absolutely perfect. Her eyes focussed on him.

"People say they want a Greek god for a hero, but a Norse god's so much better," she said dreamily.

Thor had to laugh. "I'm no god. Just a man. Your man, if you'll have me."

Her gaze dropped to his cock. "More than just a man. Most men don't last five minutes, and you've been like this for a thousand years. What are you, Thor?"

"A foundation sacrifice. A gargoyle, in your language. A protector made of living stone, sworn to keep you safe," he said. "One who's been waiting a thousand years for you."

He dropped to his knees on the bed, as she parted her thighs in welcome. He wanted to bury himself deep inside her, and forget anyone and anything else existed. Forever.

"Why me?"

He hadn't been sure at first, but now he thought he knew. "Because I am yours. Your heart and mind and beautiful body called to me, with all the power you possess, and I could not resist your call. Even a warrior like me knows when he has met his match."

No, he could not resist her. He lifted her legs up, over his shoulders, his cock poised to claim her hot, wet centre.

"Please, Thor," she begged.

So wet, so tight, so perfect…

It was his turn to moan in ecstasy as he gave her everything.

TWENTY-EIGHT

The way every bit of her ached this morning, there was no denying Thor was real, even if she'd had a shred of doubt left. Instead, Sibyl was plagued by a thousand questions, which only Thor could answer.

"So where do you go when you're not around?" Sibyl asked, stabbing another piece of waffle with her fork. She'd miss toasted waffles when she was back out at site, but that was all the more reason to get her fill of them now. "That's one of the reasons I thought you weren't real. The way you appeared and disappeared at will."

"The nature of the curse on me means I cannot stand in sunlight," Thor began. "So I could only appear to you at night, unlike inside this building, where the walls keep the sun out. While the sun shines, I go underground, which is where I was when you summoned me."

She swallowed quickly and took a mouthful of coffee to wash it down. "So, you were in an underground cave or something?"

A shadow passed across his face, like he didn't want to answer this. "No. More like a grave, filled with ice and rock and frozen soil. When you summoned me, I was able to pass through all of it to reach you."

She paused to think for a moment. "So when you came to my tent on the way here, you travelled through a whole mountain to get to me? How did you hear me through all that rock?"

He shook his head. "Not a whole mountain. When your donkey turned skittish at the beginning of your journey, I decided to follow you, through the earth beneath your feet. When you called, I was already close. In the rock beneath your tent, in fact."

"You slept under my tent? Did you do that in camp, too?"

"I do not sleep. I stand watch, guarding you."

"No sleep at all? That sounds pretty rough. If I don't get enough sleep, I need a lot of coffee to keep functioning, but you said you didn't want any. How do you survive?"

Thor chuckled, a sound that did things to her insides. Even after last night's marathon rounds of sex, she wanted more.

"It is the nature of my curse. No sunlight and no sleep and no need for sustenance, but it has allowed to me to survive for what you tell me is more than a thousand years, so that I may protect you."

He'd done a lot more than just protect her

last night. They'd used up all the condoms in the drawer – she'd have to head up to the store to get some more.

"But who curses a god? I mean, you're the god of storms and agriculture and stuff. I'd hate to meet someone who could get the best of you. That would be seriously scary."

Thor only shook his head. "I am no god. I'm merely a man, beaten in battle by an abomination that I have sworn to kill, before I was cursed by a witch. She looked like a girl from my village, not much older than my sister when the abomination killed her, but only a fool underestimates a witch. The power that girl wielded…was enough to keep me alive for a thousand years. She must have cast some sort of spell on the abomination, too, for I don't know how it could have beaten me in battle otherwise."

Sibyl thought for a long moment while she drained her coffee. She set the cup down carefully, then asked, "What exactly do you mean by an abomination? My first thought is something out of one of the games my cousin Octavia likes to play. A sort of Frankenstein's monster, a creature cobbled together from parts of different people or animals, all stitched together into a lumpy approximation of a person. A chimera, of sorts."

Thor nodded. "It is an unholy creature that is neither animal nor man, but a mixture of both. This thing was part wolf, part man, and I will defeat it, even if it takes another thousand years."

Sibyl stopped with a bite of waffle halfway to her mouth. "You mean the monster is still alive? Even after a thousand years? What if it comes to the camp? What if it comes here?" She dropped her fork back on her plate, appetite lost.

"If I live, then I have no doubt it does, too. After all, he served the same witch who cursed me. Wherever he may be, when he shows his face, rest assured that I shall protect you. I will end him, even if it is the last thing I do before the Valkyries come for me. But in order to do that, I must find my hammer. I will need every weapon I can muster to win the fight."

She believed him, or at least she believed that he believed his own words, but she wasn't sure how to break the bad news. She'd just have to spit it out, and hope for the best. "I've looked for your hammer. Karl told me it was packed with the other artefacts, but it's definitely not here. It's not in any of the boxes, and not in the store rooms, either. We must have left the box with your hammer in it at camp."

Thor rose. "Then we must depart at once."

Sibyl shook her head. "It's not that simple. For a start, I need to wait for Jakop and his donkeys. He knows the way through the mountains, and I don't. Then there's the matter of your allergy to sunlight, or whatever it is. It's morning, and there's a lot of hours of daylight left before sunset, seeing at it's June. But the good news is that it's one of the most important artefacts we've found this season, so wherever it is, Karl will make sure it's kept safe. Also…I realise you might not have thought about this, but if your hammer is as old as you are, then it's been buried under the ice for over a thousand years. While that might not have done you any damage, what with the spell you're under and everything, weapons that old aren't as strong after a thousand years as they were when they were first forged. Not to mention we've had a number of technological advancements in that time. Your hammer is a priceless artefact, far too important to be wielded as a blunt weapon in a fight, when we could go to any hardware store and pick up a sledgehammer that would probably do more damage."

He looked intrigued. "You mean to buy me a new hammer? Better than my father's weapon, the one my sister wielded in the fight that earned her a place in Valhalla, and the one I swore I would use to end the creature's life who killed her?"

Oh. Sibyl blew out a breath. Of course it was personal. No Bunnings-bought sledgehammer, however shiny and new, could replace an ancestral, storied weapon like that. Especially when it was all wrapped up in oaths of vengeance and justice and honour and stuff. She'd heard stories about Viking honour, and how highly they regarded it. If he'd vowed vengeance with his hammer, then his hammer had to deal the death blow, even if only symbolically. Like stabbing someone a hundred times until they almost bled out, then hitting them with the hammer just before their heart stopped. Or…something.

"Okay. How about…I buy you a new hammer to use temporarily, in case the monster appears, until we find your hammer. On the way back to camp, you can return that poleaxe I know you still have around here someplace. Then, when we talk to Karl and find out where your hammer is, you'll have two weapons to use against the monster." She paused. She had to ask.

Thor sighed. "You have another question, don't you, Miss Sibyl?"

She smiled ruefully. "I have a lot of

questions, actually. But this time, it's about the monster. I mean, a thousand years is a long time. Most things wouldn't live that long, and even if there is a spell protecting them, extending their life, like you, the chances of them sleeping for a thousand years and waking up at the same time seem…astronomical. Especially as I've never heard of it. So what makes you think it's still out there and that you'll finally get another shot at it?"

Thor paused for a moment. The shadow had returned, and he did not appear to want to tell her. Finally, he said, "Because I can feel its presence. It awoke when I did, and the same spell binds us to the witch. She made us protectors, and while it protects her, I must protect you."

Sibyl shivered. Maybe she should turn up the heating in here. "So the monster's coming for me?"

"No, of course not. The monster and its mistress have no knowledge of you. How could they? You were born a thousand years into the future from their time. No, it is the witch who will come seeking, and what she seeks is me. Even if she finds me, even if she tortures me, I will never tell her about you. I will keep you safe."

It should have sounded reassuring, and it did, but Sibyl couldn't help but worry. She'd seen documentaries about all sorts of things, and she knew everyone cracked under torture, eventually. Even thousand-year-old Norse gods.

"I think I'll head up to the store this morning, and see if I can get you that hammer," she said. As well as every box of condoms they had, so she didn't run out. "Any advice on what to do if I encounter your witch or her monster on the way there?"

"Hide," he said. "If you do not challenge them, or try to fight, they should not notice you, for you are no threat to them. So if you hide, and do not draw their attention, you should be safe."

Yep, that sounded like a good plan. The best they had, anyway.

TWENTY-NINE

"Who is this?" Thor asked, pointing at the back of Sibyl's laptop. It was a word he still didn't understand, except that it was the name of her strange device.

Her face flushed. "Um, that's Chris Hemsworth. From the Thor movies. People have told a lot of stories about you over the years, regarding you as a god, and a mighty hero. I'm sure most of them are made up, but it's possible that there's some truth in them. I mean, in the movies, Thor loses his hammer, just like you have. Twice, actually, if you count when his sister broke it in Ragnarok."

Thor started. "Ragnarok has already happened?"

Sibyl laughed. "Well, no, not really. It was the name of the movie."

"What is a movie?" So many words he did not understand. At least Sibyl had the patience to explain them to him.

"Uh, well, a movie is a story, told by actors. Sort of like a play, that has been captured and recorded…" She stopped. "You had storytellers in your time? People who would tell tales of heroes and great deeds and gods, and when they told the stories, sometimes they used different voices for the different people in the story?"

"Yes, of course." He'd enjoyed those as a child, though he hadn't heard many as an adult. Likely because the best storytellers had not survived Erik's attack on their village, and those who remained were not so skilled at such things.

"Well, if you imagine each person in the story being played by a different real person, acting out the events like they'd happened…and we have a sort of magic that can take a copy of the performance, so that anyone who has a copy can see the story, as these people portrayed it…" She looked at his face. "It's too much to explain, isn't it? A thousand years of technological advancement and even I don't know how to describe it, because I couldn't tell you how a camera works. My cousins could tell you – they've studied media at university."

Thor nodded. "Perhaps we could visit your family?"

Sibyl let out a shaky laugh. "Not without a plane and a passport. My family are all back home in Australia."

"I have not heard of this place. Is it far?"

"Only the other side of the world. Australia's in the Southern Hemisphere, near the Antarctic, while we're up here near the Arctic Circle."

Thor frowned. "How do you reach them without sailing off the edge of the world?"

Sibyl coughed. "Fuck. A thousand years of advancements, and I forgot about that one. How about we watch a movie, and I can show you that, at least? We can save the geography lesson for afterwards."

Thor nodded. "Sure."

THIRTY

Afterwards, Sibyl thought she probably should have found something set in Thor's time instead of the present day, but when she'd realised that the first Thor movie was the only one she'd actually downloaded onto her laptop, she figured it'd be funny to find out how Thor the man reacted to Thor the alien deity.

She'd even managed to hook her laptop up

to one of the meeting room projectors, to give the movie a more cinematic feel.

He'd been quiet at first, just watching the opening sequence with a thoughtful look on his face, and Sibyl dared to breathe again.

Then the movie cut to a Viking village in what Sibyl imagined was Thor's time. Still he said nothing, and she hoped it wasn't too different to his reality. Well, except for the two comic book alien armies, of course. That couldn't possibly have happened.

Maybe she should go to the kitchen and see if there was any popcorn. She pulled her jacket back on, ready to brave the cold in the corridor.

Thor snorted. "The handle on that hammer is far too short. The balance on such a weapon would be terrible. You'd be more likely to drop it on your own foot than hit someone in battle."

Sibyl couldn't help but agree with him. "Not like your hammer at all. The handle on that is much longer, more like the axe we used to chop wood in winter back home. Something you can swing and do some serious damage with."

He paused to stare at her. "You have seen it."

"Of course I've seen it! I'm the one who pulled it out of the ice. Where I first found you, I guess. That was your hand, wasn't it? Reaching for the hammer?" Of course it was. "We should have kept digging, instead of stopping early for dinner as soon as we found the hammer. Then you'd still have it, and when this monster you keep talking about appears, you'd know what to do."

"I do know what to do, Miss Sibyl, and if you say the hammer is back at your camp in the mountains, then we shall go there. Do you still wish to watch this movie? You seem distracted."

She sighed, and paused the film. "I've seen it before. I already know what happens. Is…is it anything like you remember?"

"Well, that man is certainly not me," he

said, pointing at the frozen Hemsworth on the screen, surrounded by Frost Giants. "I never marched into battle without Odin. While I did lead our men, it was never without his command to do so. We were like brothers, though he was older than me. As for Loki, well, those who did not know us thought all three of us brothers, we looked so alike. He was nothing like that man."

Right. So the Norse gods were just men who looked like Hemsworths. Or better than Hemsworths, if they were all like Thor.

"But Sif…she was a true warrior maiden, or she would have been, if she'd lived." Thor smiled fondly.

Sibyl had to rack her brain to remember who Sif was in the movies, as well as the mythology. "Sif was your wife?"

Thor laughed so hard he choked. "No, never! Sif had vowed never to marry, though she might have changed her mind, if she met the right man. Sif was my sister. She died in battle against that abomination when Erik attacked our village, and it is to her spirit I will dedicate the blow when I send Fenrir to Hel, where he belongs."

"Isn't Fenrir a wolf?" she ventured.

"Half wolf, half man, and all monster. He must die," Thor said.

"Right." So the stories had gotten a little garbled over the centuries. But they'd been right about his hammer… "So, this hammer of yours. Does it have any magical powers?" Sibyl asked.

Thor laughed. "You mean does it summon lightning, or make me fly? No, it is just a hammer. A tool for hitting things."

"And you're not really the god of thunder, either."

Thor tilted his head to the side. "Well, there was that one time we had a lightning storm, and I said it would not strike the village, but it would likely strike a tree on the hill above it. Moments later, a bolt of lightning split the sky, and the tree, too. My father knew how to predict the weather, and he taught me, so I always knew when a storm was coming. There was nothing magical about it, but people believed it might be, and nothing I said would persuade them otherwise. Sometimes, it's nice to believe in magic, when it will help you. Not when it's a curse that turns people into monsters."

"My cousin Callie would say that you can't turn people into monsters. They either are, or they aren't, and curses have a way of separating monsters from the rest of us. Then again, the curses she cast weren't really magic so much as…well, downright diabolical. She filled some dick's pants with chili powder once, and changed the language on his phone to Korean, because he was rude to a waitress. He turned out to be allergic to chili, and he had a terrible rash as a result." She wondered what Callie would make of this wolf monster Thor kept talking about. She was pretty sure chili was bad for dogs, too.

"Your cousin is a witch, then?"

Sibyl sighed. "Callie would say some people

call her that, but magic is just people's word for things they can't explain. She says magic doesn't really exist."

"So if you were to tell her about me, she would not believe you."

"Oh, god, no. She'd tell me I was crazy, or that you were lying. That foundation sacrifices, gargoyles like you, couldn't possibly exist." Her tone turned wistful. "I'm disappointed about the flying bit, though. I think that was the sweetest scene in the movie, where he flies off with her in his arms." Too late, she realised they hadn't watched that part yet, so Thor couldn't possibly know what she meant.

Thor snorted. "Preposterous. How anyone could believe a hammer could make a man fly. You need wings to fly. Wings like these." He rose to his feet, rolled his shoulders and…

"Fucking hell. Are those real?" Sibyl whispered.

They stretched from one wall to the other, all the way up the ceiling, like someone had stuck a giant bat to his back.

"Must I remind you again that every part of me is real, Miss Sibyl? If you wish to fly, then I shall take you." Thor held out his hand.

Sibyl didn't hesitate. She took it.

THIRTY-ONE

Thor burst through the roof, Sibyl held tightly in his arms, and spread his wings. Up, up, up, until the whole town was spread beneath them. The mountains were little more than looming shadows to the west.

"Oh, wow. That's the aurora, isn't it? I thought you couldn't see it in summer," Sibyl breathed. "It's so beautiful."

Thor spun around. Now he could see the green waves rolling across the sky. They should not be flying in this. He angled down, back toward the roof. "We should stay here, where we won't be seen," he said as they landed.

"Is it not safe to fly during an aurora?" Sibyl asked. "I've never heard that. I mean, thunderstorms are dangerous, but I thought auroras were just ionised particles from the solar wind, burning up in the upper atmosphere. Not even planes fly that high."

So many words he did not understand. Thor just shook his head. "My father told me those lights are made by the reflections off the Valkyries' armour as they ride across the bifrost, ferrying the dead from Midgard to Valhalla, and to take care not to look too closely, lest I alert them to my presence, and they take me too early. Even after a thousand years, it is too soon. I have not killed Fenrir yet."

Sibyl blinked at him. "Vikings believed the northern lights were Valkyries flying through the sky with the dead? I didn't know that."

"Not all of my people believed the lights were dangerous. When my mother heard my father's warning, she laughed and said he was silly. The lights were nothing to be afraid of. When the arctic foxes ran through the sky, their tails brushed the mountains, and sent up sparks, which were the lights we saw. There was nothing frightening about foxes playing," Thor said. To this day, he still did not know what made the lights. Maybe both foxes and Valkyries were responsible, and he would not know which one until a Valkyrie came down to claim him. He shivered. "What do your people believe?"

Sibyl laughed softly. "According to science, we're seeing particles of stardust from the sun, dancing with the air in the atmosphere until it glows. At least, that's how one of the tourist brochures described it. The tour was too expensive for me, so I figured I'd save up and try to go at the end of the year. I never realised I'd get to see the aurora out here."

Thor nodded. "Dancing stardust and foxes

playing. There are so many stories, it is hard to know what to believe any more."

He barely believed that he was here, now, with a woman in his arms he'd waited a thousand years for. A woman he would give his life for.

Sibyl squirmed around until she faced him. "Well, I believe that I'm right here, on the roof watching the aurora borealis with a gorgeous Viking, and I believe with a view this romantic, we should definitely be kissing right now."

They started with a kiss, but soon had to go back inside the building, so that he might satisfy her completely. And, by the time the sun rose, he was more than satisfied himself.

He might have only known Sibyl for a few days, but he was certain of one thing: she was the only woman for him, and he would do anything to keep her.

THIRTY-TWO

The camp had not changed at all since they had left, except that there was more snow on the ground.

"What happened to the hammer? Why didn't it make it on the supply run?" Sibyl asked.

"What do you mean? I saw Nik pack it up myself. Didn't you, Nik?"

"Of course," said a third voice. "I had to

use twice as much padding, it was so heavy. I hope you brought the replacement stuff I ordered.”

“But it wasn't there! I helped Jakop unpack everything myself, then checked all the boxes, and the hammer wasn't in any of them. It must have been left here by accident or something,” Sibyl insisted.

“You must have missed it. Because I packed it myself.”

Thor was done listening to Sibyl arguing with the two men. The hammer hadn't been in the building where he and Sibyl had stayed, which meant it must be here. If her companions hadn't seen it, then there was only one person who could have taken it.

And Thor knew exactly where to find him.

“What is wrong with you?” Loki demanded as Thor dragged him out of the ice and pinned him against a rock. “I told you I don't know where your hammer is!”

“You must have taken it! It didn't come to the town with us, so it must be here. None of the others know where it is, so you must!" Thor insisted.

"Did it ever occur to you that one of them might be lying?" Loki enquired. "Something I have never done to you, in case you've forgotten."

Thor loosened his grip on Loki's throat. The man had a point. For all the pranks Loki liked to play, he had never actually lied to him. In fact, the few times Loki had taken something from him, he'd gloated loudly about how he knew where it was and Thor would never find it. So if Loki wasn't gloating now…

"But which one?" Thor asked.

Loki shoved him away and brushed off his tunic. "How should I know? I don't have anything to do with them. Unlike you and your little witch. Don't think I didn't see you kissing her while the others weren't looking…"

"Sibyl. Her name is Sibyl, and if you so much as look at her wrong, I will smash your face with my fist," Thor threatened.

"Right, right. You're her protector, and all

that. Some protector you are, without a weapon."

Thor considered telling him about the poleaxe, but Sibyl had insisted he put it back, so he had. She would not be pleased if he dug it up again. She'd bought him a shiny new hammer, but he'd left it with her things at the laboratory. The balance just didn't feel right, and he hadn't the heart to tell her. He needed his hammer.

"Then help me find it, Loki!"

Loki tapped his lips. "Well, I might be able to help you, if you help me. You see, I promised I'd help someone search people's tents, but in order to do that, someone has to distract everyone and keep them away long enough to do a thorough search. If you and your witch friend can make a distraction, I can let you know if we find anything."

Thor thought for a moment. "Do it now. I will hold everyone's attention for as long as I can," he said.

THIRTY-THREE

"I found it!" Thor burst into the tent, bottle in hand, with a beaming smile upon his face.

Sibyl's jaw dropped.

"Who in blazes are you?" Nik snapped.

"I'm Thor. Sibyl's friend. I said I'd meet her here when I found where I'd stashed the bottle of mead and I found it!" He brandished the bottle. "Now, we need to warm it up properly, and we need glasses for everybody. Everybody must drink a toast to our handfasting!" As he drew close enough to lean in to kiss her cheek, he whispered, "Must keep them all in here for as long as possible." Then he raised his voice to its normal volume. "With Sibyl's family so far away, we wanted you, as her friends and colleagues, to be part of the ceremony. Who is the leader here?"

Karl and Lara exchanged glances. Lara was the one who spoke first. "Well, Karl is the expedition leader…"

"But Lara is the one who makes sure everything runs smoothly, so it should really be you," Karl said.

"Excellent! Both of you can perform the ceremony!" Thor said.

Lara looked doubtful. "But I've never done one before, and it's not like searching it up on the internet will be easy out here."

"I have seen it done many times. All you must do is bind our hands together, and ask us to say the vows. Then we are handfasted, and we drink!" Thor said.

Lara still wasn't convinced. She looked at Sibyl. "Are you sure about this?"

Of course not. She'd never had a boyfriend for more than a few months, and this was…commitment. How could this Norse god possibly want to be tied to her?

"I have never been more certain of anything in my life! Sibyl is the kindest, loveliest woman I have ever met, and I am honoured that she chose to spend a year with me. I only hope that it is time enough to convince her let me protect and cherish her forever!"

He meant it. He really meant it.

Sibyl swallowed. Time to make shit up, then, and really sell this. Everyone's eyes were on her. "Yes, handfasting. Thor said it's an old Viking custom. Agreeing to be together for a year. Kind of like a betrothal or living together. We decided to do it while we were in town, but he said there's usually a celebration with friends to mark the ceremony, and seeing as everyone's out here, I told him he'd have to come with me to camp if he wanted to meet everyone, so… here he is. But one bottle of mead won't be enough for everyone. We should go back to my tent and find some more." She gave Thor a significant glance and jerked her head toward the door.

Thor shook his head. "I'm sure this will be plenty! We can get more later. Help me find the glasses, Sibyl."

"I'll go get the rest. Be right back," Jorunn said cheerfully, slipping out the door before Sibyl could stop her.

Thor didn't appear to be concerned. Perhaps he just wanted everyone else to stay? Sibyl would do her best.

Lara sidled up to Thor. "Sibyl never told us she had a boyfriend back in civilisation. Where'd she meet you?"

"I went out one night, and he offered to walk me home. We got to talking, and found we had a lot in common – a shared interest in Viking history and weapons, for a start. Oh, and wait until Jorunn comes back…he's worked with reindeer! But enough about us.

Thor, pour the mead. Tell us what you've found while I've been gone!"

Sibyl pasted a smile on her face and did her best to say as little as possible about Thor as the others told her about their progress on the site. Arrows, animal bones and a child's shoe seemed to be all they'd found, but Sibyl kept asking for more details, drawing it out, as Thor poured the drinks so slowly, she might have sworn it was pitch instead of mead.

Finally he was done.

He pulled a length of ribbon out of a pouch strapped to his belt and held it up. "This belonged to my sister. She said if I were ever to be handfasted, I must use this ribbon for luck."

A lump formed in Sibyl's throat. From the way he talked about his late sister, that ribbon must be very precious to him. If he intended to use it now, he was absolutely serious about this. Could she agree to be his partner for a year?

Well, the sex was already amazing. He was

funny, and he wanted to protect her. They had a shared interest in Viking history, even if it wasn't exactly history to him. Besides, he'd said he was sworn to serve her, because she'd summoned him. She couldn't even begin to understand how that worked, but that meant she wasn't going to be getting rid of him any time soon, handfasting or no handfasting. Plus, she'd never met a man more easy on the eyes…

Thor handed the precious piece of ribbon to Lara. "You must bind our hands with this, while you – " He pointed at Karl. " – ask us to say the vows. Once we have said the words, we must share a cup of mead, and remain bound together until everyone has toasted our handfasting. Then we may remove the ribbon, but it cannot be cut or damaged, or the same will happen to our relationship," Thor finished.

So she was supposed to get tied up, get drunk, and then Thor had to help her untie herself. Nothing could possibly go wrong with that.

Lara looked at the ribbon and made her decision. "All right, then, how do we do this?"

"You both stand here." Thor pointed. He seized Sibyl's hand in his and pulled her to his side. "We shall stand here, and you may begin."

Oh, fuck. They were definitely doing this.

He held their clasped hands out, and Lara began to wrap the ribbon around them. Thousand-year-old silk, as soft as if it had been spun yesterday. It belonged in a museum, for all the world to see, not around her bare hand. And yet…this ribbon was something personal and precious to Thor, so he was the one who got to decide what to do with it. For some reason she did not understand, he wanted to use it to bind them together. And she wanted…well, him, obviously, but…

"Is that tight enough, or do I need to do it again?" Lara asked anxiously. She'd finished wrapping the ribbon around them, and tied the ends into a little bow. That shouldn't be too hard to untie, so they wouldn't damage it. Sibyl allowed herself to breathe again.

"That's wonderful." Thor beamed at Lara, then turned the same devastating smile on Sibyl. "Are you ready?" He reached over to capture her other hand, too.

Her hand. Her breath. Her heart. Her…nope, her knickers had definitely melted this time. She was ready to jump him and pin him to the wall, even with all these people watching. She definitely shouldn't do that. Wait, what was it he'd asked her?

"Are you ready, ástin mín?"

My love. And the way he was looking at her, his eyes burning into her very soul…

Her throat turned dry. Unable to get any words out, Sibyl just nodded.

"Time for the vows, then!"

Karl cleared his throat. "Uh, Thor, do you agree to a handfasting with this woman?"

"I, Thor, Hymir's son, vow to love, honour and protect this woman, and fight at her side for a year from this day."

Karl seemed to relax into the role a little. "Okay, Sibyl, do you agree?"

Thor squeezed her hands, his gaze never leaving hers. He wanted this. Wanted her. And she…fuck, who was she kidding? If His Norse Hotness was willing, she'd keep him forever, not just for a year.

Sibyl took a deep breath. "I, Sibyl, Cassandra's daughter, vow to love, honour and protect this man, and fight at his side for a year from this day."

Thor's grin couldn't have gotten any wider. But then he leaned in to kiss her, and she forgot everything else.

Well, until the cheers and cries of "Get a room!" got too loud to ignore.

"Now, we must share a cup of mead," Thor said.

"I'll get you one!" Lara said, holding out a cup.

With Thor holding both her hands, Sibyl wasn't sure how this was supposed to work.

Luckily, Thor wasn't as clueless. He reached

forward with their bound hands, so both his and her fingers curled around the cup.

"I'll drink first," he said, lifting the cup to his lips. A long moment passed, before he wiped his mouth with the back of his free hand and held the cup out to Sibyl.

Just as she suspected, he hadn't drunk more than a drop.

"We must finish it all," Thor said.

Of course they did.

Sibyl drank deeply, feeling the burn as the warm mead slid down her throat. There was so much of it, and her head was swimming. But with Thor's eyes on her, so expectant and trusting, she made herself drink it all. Finally, the cup was empty.

"Another!"

A second cup was forced into her free hand, as everyone else collected a glass, too.

"To the handfasting of Thor and Sibyl!"

By the time she'd finished the second cup, accepting congratulations and hugs from everyone, she was having trouble staying on her feet. Luckily, she was still tied to Thor, whose arm around her waist kept her from falling.

That's when Jorunn returned. "I don't know where you put the rest of the mead, but I couldn't find any!"

Thor's grip tightened around Sibyl's waist. "Don't worry, we'll go find it. We'll be right back."

He hurried her across the camp to her tent.

The featherlight brush of something on her wrist drew her attention to the ribbon, which Thor had already untied and was now carefully storing back in its pouch. "Gods willing, we will use it again in a year, when we are wed."

She stared at him. He meant this, too.

But none of this made any sense. Handfasting, marriage, all of it. Not to mention…

"There isn't any more mead. I only bought the one bottle!" Sibyl hissed. "We can't go back in there without more mead!"

"It does not matter. In a traditional

handfasting, the couple usually leave the feast early to engage in a more intimate celebration. The mead is merely an excuse."

Well, they'd have the tent to themselves, at least, with Jorunn still in the mess tent. But everyone would hear them…

"What matters is that the search is finished," Thor finished, nodding at a shadowy figure waiting beside the tent.

Sibyl's blood ran cold, sobering her up almost instantly.

"Who are you?" Sibyl asked, looking the new man up and down. He was dressed like Thor, but way more wiry. Like he was Thor's younger brother, which couldn't be possible. Thor had said he had no family left.

"Loki," Thor growled in warning.

The man closed his eyes and sighed. "Your betrothed said if I so much as looked at you wrong, he would punch me. As I don't want to offend, here." He shoved something into her hands. "We didn't find a hammer, but we did find this. I hope it means more to you than it does to me." He stalked off into the darkness.

Sibyl looked down. "Why am I holding a satphone?" She brought it closer to her headlamp. "This isn't Lara's one. It's smaller." She pressed a button, and the screen lit up. "Looks like someone's been taking pictures of the waste barrels." Why anyone would do that, she had no idea. Maybe it was a mistake, and there were better pictures further along. "A whole gallery of barrels and…wait, is that your hammer? It looks like the handle…" She peered closer. "It went in one of the waste barrels to keep it safe, because it was too big for any of the boxes! We have to go back to the lab before the waste company comes to dispose of them. If only Jakop hadn't already left…"

"We don't need donkeys to get there. I can fly you over the mountains before morning, if we leave now," Thor said.

"I can't just leave…" she began, but she also couldn't risk sending that precious hammer and her PhD to the nearest landfill, either. "I'll tell Karl you're an experienced hiker, and that we left something at the lab, so we have to go back and get it. I'll tell him we'll catch up with Jakop and travel the rest of the way with him."

THIRTY-FOUR

"Quick, get inside before the sun's up," Sibyl said, pushing Thor through the door before following him into the cramped vestibule. She was half dead on her feet, after flying all night with Thor, but he had to be exhausted, seeing as he'd been the one actually doing the flying, while she'd just been along for the ride.

"We need to make sure the hammer's here," he said.

She sighed. "All right, I'll go check to see if the waste barrels are still here. We can check the contents in the morning."

She lurched across the yard to the shed, where an open padlock dangled from the door. She tugged it out of the bolt and opened the door. It took her a lot of fumbling before she managed to turn on her headlamp, but as the beam played over the stacked barrels, she dared to breathe again. The hammer was here. It had to be.

Sibyl closed the door and clicked the padlock into place.

She returned to the lab building, where she found Thor sitting expectantly in the cafeteria. "The barrels are all still here. No one's come to pick them up yet. We can check them tonight."

"But if my hammer's there…" he began eagerly.

She set a hand on his chest, before almost toppling over onto him. "I need to sleep, Thor. I'm no help to you like this, and you can't go out in the sun, remember. So if you're stuck here until sunset, the least you can do is let me sleep until we can go out there together. I promise I'll help you get your hammer back. I'm just…not an immortal Viking gargoyle Norse god…" Then the world sort of slid sideways.

Luckily, Thor caught her before she hit the floor.

"Of course, Miss Sibyl."

THIRTY-FIVE

It was past lunchtime when Sibyl finally woke up. Thor was nowhere to be seen, but as it was still daylight outside, she figured he'd reappear by the time the sun went down. She considered searching through the barrels herself until she found his hammer, but she'd barely been able to lift the hammer when they'd first found it, and now it was packed in a barrel with who knew how much padding and other stuff to protect it, she'd definitely need Thor's help to get it out. Not to mention there were a lot of barrels in there, which she'd need help moving them until she found the right one.

Poor Thor. It must really suck not being able to go out in the sun. To know his hammer was so close, and yet still out of reach for a few more hours. Maybe there was a way to break the curse. Not that she knew much about witchcraft or magic, but she knew someone who did.

Unfortunately, Callie wasn't answering her phone.

Sibyl tried three times, but still no answer. Maybe Callie was in a lecture, with her phone on silent. She'd try again later.

Next, she called Catena. As a fellow archaeologist, Catena had worked on a few different sites, like Sibyl, but her godmother Maria was a legend in the archaeology community who'd worked all over the world. If anyone had come across gargoyles or foundation sacrifices on a dig, it was Maria.

Of course, she didn't have Catena's number in her phone. It should be in her email somewhere, though…

Her email inbox was overflowing. Even after Sibyl had deleted all the spam, there were still heaps to skim through. A search for Catena's name brought up an email from Callie, so Sibyl clicked on it. And nearly lost it laughing.

A Moth Man? Seriously? It wasn't as hot as digging up a Norse god, or near enough, but…

Sibyl clicked on the video link. It kind of looked like a guy in a Batman suit with wings, but if she squinted, he also looked a little like Thor. Not that she'd ever seen Thor dance. Did Vikings dance?

Then again, what were the chances of one of her friends finding a gargoyle at the same time that she had? She had to call Catena.

On the third email, she hit paydirt — Catena's number, at the bottom of her email signature.

Unlike Callie, Catena answered on the first ring.

"Hello?" she ventured.

"Cat! It's so good to hear your voice!"

A long pause. "Is that Sibyl?"

"That's me! Fresh from the frozen wastes of the Arctic, back in civilisation for a little while before they send me back to site with the next load of supplies."

Sibyl found herself babbling about life in camp, and how much of a dick Saint Nik was, though everyone else was wonderful. The problem was, she wasn't sure how to shift the subject around to Thor, or the Moth Man.

Finally, she paused to take a breath.

"It sounds amazing," Catena admitted.

Well, now or never. "I haven't even told you the best part! I've…"

Found a thousand-year-old Viking god and he's amazing in bed.

Nope.

Somehow unearthed a cursed Viking warrior and I want to know what you know about curses.

Hell no.

Heard you got captured by a paranormal creature and I want to compare notes.

Definitely not.

Sibyl chickened out. "I've…met someone…and I'll probably be staying for another season, to see what else we can find. I'm learning so much."

Silence. Catena never had been much of a gossip. Not like the others. Callie would be asking how big Thor's dick was by now.

Enormous and so, so addictive.

Sibyl swallowed. "How about you? Have you decided on a PhD project yet, or did Alethea talk you into joining her company as a consultant instead?"

Catena blew out a breath that sounded awfully frustrated. "I'm finalising my project proposal this week. I definitely want to do my PhD next year, and no, Alethea hadn't managed to talk me into digging up dead bodies with her. Did you know their latest project was digging up an old colonial cemetery?" Sibyl imagined Catena shuddering. She was a great archaeologist, but she didn't want anything to do with dead bodies.

Sibyl smothered a laugh. Good thing Catena wasn't here in Norway. "Well, you know that's the holy grail up here. Dead bodies. Frozen ones. They're hoping to find another ice mummy like Otzi. My friend says we have a good chance of finding one, too, because it was an ancient trading and raiding route. Thor knows so much about Viking history…"

Oops. She probably shouldn't have mentioned Thor. Well, too late now. She should change the subject quickly.

"Anyway, what about you? Have you met anyone yet? And what's this I hear about you having a major moth problem? I tried to watch the video, but I only saw a few seconds of his moves before the video froze. The internet connection here keeps dropping out. It might feel like civilisation after the dig site, but it's really just a few storage rooms and a lab, on the outskirts of a tiny town. So, are you going to tell me about him?"

More silence. Sibyl wondered if the call had dropped out.

Finally, Catena said, "There's nothing to tell, really. Just a silly video of a guy in a coat they're making out to be a monster. He's not, honestly. He's the sweetest, most chivalrous guy I've ever met. He's…" Another pause. "We're just friends," she finished.

Sibyl wasn't buying that for a second.

"Uh huh. Sure. Just like me and Thor. I want to know where he learned to dance like that. I expect to meet him when I get home. Or we can video call when we're done. I want to hear every single detail."

"Miss Sibyl? It's sunset."

Sibyl's mind went blank at the sight of Thor in little more than his short kilt, standing in the doorway. She wanted to take him back to bed and ravish him.

But first, they needed to find his missing hammer. She had promised.

"Sorry, Cat, I have to go. Thor said one of the artefacts is missing, and it's really important. Talk later. Bye."

She ended the call and gave Thor her full attention. "Right. Let's get suited up so we can find your hammer."

Thor frowned. "Suited up? What does that mean?"

"Well, I don't know about you, but I'm not going through barrels of waste without my biohazard suit on. They're in the cupboard outside the necropsy lab, where we keep all the bones." At Thor's look of complete and utter confusion, she took pity on him. Translation magic couldn't keep up with technology. "Here, I'll show you. I'm sure there'll be a suit in your size." Most of the men on the expedition were Viking sized, so something had to fit him.

But when she opened the cupboard, all the hooks were empty except for three: the one for Sibyl's suit, alongside the ones for Jorunn and Freyja, the lab manager. Jorunn's suit was long enough, but there was no way it was wide enough for Thor's shoulders. Freyja's one, though…that looked like it had been made for a tall woman with distinctive curves.

It was a bit of a squeeze, but Thor managed to get into Freyja's suit, even if he did chunter under his breath a bit as he kept adjusting it. "Are you sure this is necessary?" he asked.

Now he didn't look like His Norse Hotness so much as a giant white frowning marshmallow man.

Sibyl ducked her head to hide her smile as she fastened the seals on her own suit. Hers wasn't comfortable, either, but at least hers was custom made to her measurements. "You want your hammer back, don't you?"

He gave a curt nod.

"Think of it as armour for going into battle," Sibyl suggested. Armour that would help block out the smell, she thought but didn't say.

"Women's clothing is not armour. Women are to be protected. They should not have to fight," Thor grumbled.

Scratch the man and reveal the inner misogynist. So much about fighting at each other's side when they got handfasted. Sibyl just shook her head. "Didn't you say your sister fought with that hammer, and is now in Valhalla? Isn't that place just for warriors?"

Thor frowned. "She should not have had to fight. I should have been there to protect her when they came."

Maybe it wasn't so much misogyny as guilt. A thousand years was a long time to carry such a burden. "Didn't you also say the same monster who killed her also defeated you? Even if you'd been there for the initial attack, could you have saved her?"

"I…I would have tried," he said grudgingly. "At least I would have died with honour, defending her."

Survivor's guilt. Sibyl had heard about this one. "Well, you're not dead yet, so you still have a chance at that glorious death in battle. Do you want your hammer back for it, or not?"

"I will not go into battle against the abomination without it," he said. "I owe her that much."

"Right. So, are you ready to march into battle to find it, then?"

Another curt nod. "Even if I must dress like a woman to do it."

Sibyl had to laugh. "You know men wear suits like this, too. When mine arrived, Karl said he was due to order a new one. At least these ones are white. The ones they're using in some parts of the world for the pandemic are bright orange."

Thor still didn't look convinced, but he did look ready to go, so Sibyl led the way out to the barrel shed.

The number of barrels had doubled while she'd slept – evidently Jakop had brought in another load. "Those ones are new. The ones we want are the row against the wall. Can you help me move them out of the way, so we can reach them?"

Thor didn't so much help as move them all, as most of them were too heavy for her to budge. Having a Norse god around was definitely useful.

"Right. So we just need to open these and check what's inside. If you see anything that looks like the padding in that picture, give a shout," Sibyl said, looking for something to use to pry the barrels open. There were a couple of crowbars in the corner, but she settled for a particularly chunky screwdriver.

The first one she pried open looked to be filled with dirty ice and slush. She quickly closed that back up again before the smell seeped out. The next two were filled with what looked like food scraps and rubbish from the mess tent. "Wow, we sure do eat a lot of fish," she said, moving on to the next barrel.

"Hey, this one has a letter on it. It looks sort of like a P, or maybe a D," she said.

Even through the bulky suits, she could feel Thor looming over her. "It looks like my mark, which is also the mark for danger. It's the rune thurs. But I did not make this mark."

"So…do you think we should open it? If someone took the effort to mark this barrel as dangerous, maybe we should leave this one."

"Did you not say these silly suits would protect us like armour? You may stand back, but I will open it. Danger or not, this cask bears my mark, so it follows that what it contains is mine!"

Yet as Thor pried at the lid with his crowbar, Sibyl couldn't make herself stand back. It wasn't like she expected to find anything worse than she'd already seen today. He lifted the lid, and Sibyl's breath caught in her throat at the sight of the same sort of wadding that filled the boxes in the lab. This was it. It had to be.

He tore into the wadding like a toddler opening a birthday present. The tinkle of something small and metallic hitting the concrete rang out.

"Wait, stop!" she said, darting forward to catch the cascade. It wasn't one item, but more than a dozen of what looked like brooches and coins, stuff she'd never seen before. "Where did all this come from?" she asked, picking up a large, golden piece as big as the palm of her hand. When she turned it over, she realised it was just the setting that was gold, framing a huge piece of amber that seemed to glow.

Thor growled. "This belonged to Odin's wife. A wedding gift from her family. From the day she died, he never took it off."

"Maybe someone put it in here to keep it safe," Sibyl suggested, but the words felt wrong. Everything in the boxes had been carefully packed for the journey across the mountains, and she'd made sure they were stored safely in the lab. Someone had hidden the jewels here.

She gathered them all up and wrapped them carefully in the piece of wadding they'd fallen from, then placed the bundle on top of one of the new barrels. "Okay, now you can remove more of the padding, but carefully, in case there's other artefacts in there."

Thor reached into the barrel, but this time the bundle he pulled out was a big one. The big one. If this wasn't Thor's hammer, Sibyl would eat nothing but raw herring for the rest of the summer.

He laid his bundle across the top of two barrels, and began to unwrap it with far more care.

Sibyl couldn't smother her gasp as the final layer came away. The hammer head shone like modern steel, or silver at the very least. It didn't look a thousand years old – it looked brand new. The leather-wrapped handle looked like it had seen some use, though it didn't look particularly worn. Like it was a ceremonial weapon, only used for the most important of occasions.

Thor flexed his gloved hands, then wrapped them around the hammer's handle. In one mighty stroke, he smashed the empty barrel flat, sending an explosion of paperwork flying in all directions. "How dare you try to conceal my hammer from me!" he roared, raising the hammer to pulverise the debris.

Sibyl rushed forward to stop him. If he destroyed any of the other barrels, things could get very messy, very quickly. Besides, those papers could be important. "Stop, stop! You can't go smashing things indiscriminately like that. I know you're happy to have your hammer back. Let's take it inside so we can get out of these awful suits, and I can put those other artefacts away. Oh, and will you help me gather up these papers?"

While Thor hefted the hammer proudly over his shoulder, Sibyl tucked the bundle of jewellery and papers under her arm.

It wasn't until she'd changed out of her suit and laid her finds out on one of the lab tables that she realised the significance of her little hoard. "These are the artefact tags for all of these things, including your hammer." Quickly, she matched each tag to the piece it belonged to, before packing everything into one of the empty boxes. That left only one sheet – the one for Thor's hammer.

"I do not like hazmat suits," Thor announced as he sauntered into the lab, still holding his hammer. He'd left his cloak behind, so there was plenty of bare skin to hold her gaze, between his kilt and boots and shoulder guards. A normal man should be wearing a shirt and a whole lot more warm clothing, but she knew from experience that if she pressed a hand to Thor's chest, he'd be every bit as warm as she was, with no need to cover up.

Nothing beat a Norse god.

"Miss Sibyl, I owe you a great deal for helping me find my hammer. How would you like me to show my gratitude?"

Her mouth went dry. Was it wrong to ask him to pose naked for her with just his hammer? Just one photo. Or maybe two, in case one pose looked hotter than the other. Or…

His eyes glinted with mischief. "I believe we should retire to your bedchamber for what you have in mind."

Moments later, the hammer lay forgotten on the desk, as Thor pounded her pussy with a far more pleasurable weapon, and she cried out for joy. Who needed pictures when she had him?

THIRTY-SIX

The next morning, Sibyl's legs ached in places they'd never done before. She probably shouldn't have ridden him so hard, but when he'd begged her to take a turn on top, they'd both enjoyed it so much that he'd taken hold of her hips, to prolong their shared pleasure, and...

Fuck, he was an absolute god in bed, for all that he said he was just a man. Her poor pussy would never want a mortal man again, after Thor.

Unless there was a way to break the curse so Thor could be a normal man again. Well, hardly normal, but…

She tried calling Callie again, but still got no answer.

So she called Tacey instead. May as well call all her cousins while she had a moment. It would be lovely to catch up and find out what they were doing.

"Hello?" Tacey sounded suspicious.

"Tacey? Is that you? It's Sibyl!"

She heard a chorus of cries at that, like Tacey wasn't alone.

"Who's there?" Sibyl asked.

"I have you on speaker, because I'm home with Rory, Octavia, Alethea, Callie and Rochelle."

Jackpot. Not that she could say much in front of five-year-old Rory, but…

"Oh, perfect! So I can tell all of you – I met someone up here, a real Viking, so I'm staying for another season so we can work on this dig together. We've already found so much, but we're hoping for an ice mummy, like Otzi. Seeing as the borders are still closed, it's probably the best place for me, until it's safe to come home. We're pretty isolated, so we've missed the worst of the pandemic in the big cities so far. Even now I'm in civilisation, it's a tiny little town, and half of it's taken up by our research labs. Can you believe there's still snow on the ground in summer?"

"It was like that in Scotland sometimes," someone said. A male voice Sibyl didn't recognise.

"Who was that? Who else is there? Has one of you finally gotten a boyfriend?" Sibyl demanded.

"Well, Octavia's engaged, and her and Callie are considering a double wedding when the weather gets warmer and the restrictions ease," Tacey said.

Sibyl let out a squeal. "What? Oh, I want to be there. Callie and Octavia getting married?

And here I thought you or Alethea would be first…"

Hell, she should tell them about getting handfasted to Thor. But how did you tell your family something like that?

Luckily, Alethea got in first. "What about you? Did you say you'd met someone in the Arctic? Is he hot?"

Sibyl swallowed.

"Didn't I tell you? Oh, you have to meet Thor. He's a real, live Viking, just like they made them a thousand years ago. I'd take him over a Hemsworth any day, because he's the real deal. Oh, did you say Callie's there?"

"I'm here!" Callie called, sounding like she was in the bottom of a well, or at least not that close to the phone.

Sibyl took a deep breath. "Hey, in all your research on ancient spells and stuff, did you ever run into mentions about foundation sacrifices, or gargoyles?"

Silence.

Shit. They'd never believe her if she told

them the truth about Thor, not if she'd shocked them with just a mention of what he was. She should never have called them.

As if by magic, her phone beeped with a message.

"Oh, wait, I've just got an emergency message coming through…" Sibyl said, swiping across to see what she'd been sent.

The message was from Lara's satellite phone.

Her jaw dropped, and it took her a long moment before she could speak again.

"Um, we were supposed to ship out in a week, with the next supply run, but they've found something in the glacier that needs to be helicoptered to the lab right away, which means I need to get out to the helipad if I want a ride. It might be a body buried in the ice - a real live Viking!" The moment the words left her lips, she regretted them. Of course the ice mummy they'd found couldn't possibly be alive. He wasn't Thor.

She hurried to end the call so she could tell

Thor they were headed back to camp.

THIRTY-SEVEN

"If they have found someone, it must be Odin," Thor said when Sibyl told him the news.

Sibyl's mind blanked for a moment. "You mean...Odin, Odin? The father of all the Norse gods, rides an eight-legged horse, traded his eye for wisdom, Odin?"

Thor laughed. "I mean the leader of our village, Odin. He's no more a god than I am.

But if his wife's brooch was there, then he could not have been far. If your people have found his body, then he was buried with full honours, and his soul likely resides in Valhalla, as was his due." He looked thoughtful for a moment. "Wherever did you hear that about Sleipnir?"

"Sleipnir? Oh, you mean his horse? It's part of the Norse myths. Odin had a horse that could travel with unusual swiftness, on its eight legs. There are also rumours that Loki was its mother…" Even Sibyl found that one hard to believe. There were trans people in the present, but she couldn't imagine things would have been the same a thousand years ago. Hormone treatments and surgery would have been non-existent, for a start.

"Of all the details to survive for a thousand years…Loki was Sleipnir's mother, or at least the horse thought so. He found the foal beside its dead mother, and he raised it. The creature did not have any more than the normal number of legs, but he did run uncommonly fast. Loki was never much of a rider, and after the beast tossed him off a couple of times, Loki gave him to Odin. He never bucked Odin off, that's for sure."

Sibyl could only shake her head, as they walked up to the reception desk at the tiny airport that served the town.

"You are here for the helicopter, yes?" the woman behind the desk asked.

"Yes. Flying across the mountains to the archaeology dig for the university," Sibyl said. She pointed to herself and Thor. "Both of us."

She expected the woman to protest, but she just shot Thor an admiring glance and nodded. At least he'd bundled the hammer up in his cloak, instead of carrying the weapon openly.

"The pilot is ready to take off when you are. Do you have any luggage?"

Sibyl shook her head. She'd left everything back at camp.

"I tell him you are ready to go, then?"

All too soon, they'd climbed aboard the helicopter, which looked like it could easily take a dozen more passengers than just the two of them. The only time Sibyl had seen helicopters this big was up in Broome and the Pilbara, ferrying staff out to the offshore oil and gas rigs. More than big enough to take an ice encrusted body back to the lab – even if he'd been as big as Thor in life.

Sibyl had to help Thor with his safety harness, because he'd never seen anything like it before. It took her a moment to work out how to fasten her own, but the pilot was too busy doing his pre-flight checks to care much about his passengers. Also, it turned out he was waiting for a carton of French champagne that Karl had ordered. He'd been waiting a long time to find his ice man, and now he'd finally found one, Karl evidently wanted to celebrate.

The pilot handed out headphones, like they did on charter flights back home. Sibyl considered making a joke about the inflight movie, until she realised Thor didn't know what to do with his headphones, and she needed to help him before the pilot noticed anything strange about his passengers.

Takeoff was…phenomenal. She'd never been in a helicopter before, and there was so much more to see outside than through the tiny porthole windows on a plane. In fact, she was the one behaving like a first-time tourist, while Thor just sat back with a smile on his face, watching her.

That's when she realised he was used to flying, what with having wings and all.

Bloody smug Norse Hotness.

The flight was over far too soon, as the twinkling lights of the camp came into view, beside the temporary helipad they'd created with a ring of lights. Just like they did at remote site air strips back home. Only at home, the lights weren't reflected by ice and snow.

The pilot shooed them out of his helicopter, depositing the box of champagne in Thor's arms, before turning to greet the rest of the expedition team.

Four men – it was too dark to see their faces – carried what Sibyl could only describe as a body bag. It evidently took all four of them to lift it into the helicopter, and secure it to the middle of the cabin, between the rows of seats. Then they returned for a second body bag, and laid it beside the first.

Then they all climbed out, except for the pilot, and the helicopter flew off with its precious cargo.

"Let's take this to the mess tent," Karl said, taking the box from Thor.

Sibyl was surprised Karl hadn't gone with the ice mummy. It was his dream find, after all.

Lara must have thought the same thing, because when they trooped into the mess tent, she said, "What? Not flying back to civilisation with your baby to make sure they take care of him?"

Karl just laughed. "Freyja's on her way up to the lab right now. She'll take the delivery. He couldn't be in better hands. She is a doctor, after all."

Lara had already set out cups – the same ones they'd used for the mead – so Karl popped open the first bottle and started pouring.

When everyone had a glass, he raised his. "To Odin!"

They all repeated the toast, and drank. Sibyl searched the tent for Thor, but he'd vanished.

How did they know it was Odin, then, if Thor hadn't told them? And who was in the second body bag?

She sidled up to Karl. "Why are you calling him Odin? Did he have a name badge on him?" Like Thor had worn the suit with Freyja's name badge on it last night.

Karl laughed. "No. He was still too deep in the ice for us to see much of him, but he had a patch over one eye and a spear in his hand, so it seemed a good enough name for an important man. I'm sure the university will name him properly, so it doesn't matter what we call him. Ah, but your glass is empty. Let me get you more champagne! Not only will you have the hammer to research, but an entire Viking grave to investigate for your PhD! Never have we had such a successful season, and it's not even halfway through. You and Jorunn are our lucky charms."

"You mean…Jorunn found the ice mummy?"

Sibyl shouldn't have been so surprised. It could have been any of them, really, seeing as they walked the grid in a search pattern. Better Jorunn than Saint Nik.

She glanced around. Jorunn was clinking glasses with Lara, looking like they were intent on some sort of drinking game, while the three men she couldn't tell apart cheered them on. Karl beamed like a Christmas lantern… "Where's Nik?" she blurted out.

A tiny crease appeared in Karl's forehead. "Ah, there was a terrible accident. Nik went walking outside the camp at night and was attacked by an animal. He was terribly injured and we had to send him to hospital in the helicopter."

The second body bag. "He's dead?" Sibyl cried. She might not have liked him, but he didn't deserve to die just for being an arsehole.

The crease vanished. "No, no! He is alive, but injured. The animal attack. He will recover." Karl managed a rueful smile. "If he had not been injured, we might never have found the ice man. We shall save a bottle for Nik, I think." He hurried off to get to the champagne before it was all gone.

THIRTY-EIGHT

Thor left Sibyl and her friends merrily drinking in the feasting tent, and went to find Loki.

"I see you found your hammer."

Of course, Loki was the one to find him, appearing in the darkness like he'd sprung out of the ice. Perhaps he had.

"I did. Now, I am ready to defend Sibyl from all threats, even if the witch and her wolf return." Thor squinted at him. "Is it true that they have found Odin's grave?"

"What do you mean his grave? He was cursed right along with us. You don't get a grave until you're dead. Do you feel dead?"

Thor gaped. "Odin is alive?"

"Of course he's alive. Just frozen in the ice. I wonder what he'll do when he wakes up?" Loki grinned, mischief lighting his eyes.

"But they are going to…do tests on him. Examine him. Sibyl said they will even scan him. That is what they do to dead bodies they find in the ice, so they can learn more about history. They can't do that if he is alive!" Actually, Thor wasn't sure what most of those things were, but Sibyl had talked about them non stop with a great deal of excitement, as she spoke of doing the same things to his hammer.

Loki's grin only widened. "I'm sure he'll tell them."

Thor shook his head. "But this is an important discovery to Sibyl and her friends. They wish to learn about the past, and they have been looking for a body to conduct these tests on. She will be terribly disappointed, and so will the others."

Loki shrugged. "They'll get over it. There are other bodies beneath the ice. Scores of them, and the rest of them are actually dead. What do you think happened to the rest of our warriors? Only you, me and Odin were cursed. The others just died and were buried beside Odin. They made him stand and watch before they cursed him. All of them just thrown into a pit with all their weapons all jumbled up together. I can just imagine them all trying to grab their weapons, all at the same time, when the Valkyries came to claim them."

Thor strode toward the sounds of merriment. "Then we must tell the others, and guide them to the spot where they can find these bodies. Before they are disappointed by finding out Odin is not dead."

Loki held up his hands. "Oh, you're on your own on that one. You're the one sworn to serve. I don't see the need to be helpful at all."

Of course he did not. Loki like chaos too much for that. But that didn't stop Thor.

He swept into the tent, surprising all of them. "Is it true? You found an important warrior?"

The oldest man among them, the one who'd helped with the handfasting, who now stood beside Sibyl with a drink in his hand, nodded. "Definitely an important man. A very ornate burial, from what we can see."

"Then you must look very carefully at the soil surrounding his grave. His men would have fought beside him, and they would have been buried nearby, for a leader rarely dies alone. I have seen a number of such graveyards, and the pattern is always the same."

Thor took a sheet of paper and one of the pencils Sibyl liked to use and began to draw. "The leader would be here, and his men…" He sketched them in quickly, based on what Loki had told him of their whereabouts. "Can you show me where you found Odin?"

Karl slapped Thor on the back. "Of course! You must come and see!" Grabbing an open bottle, which he tucked under his arm, he led the way out of the tent. "Sibyl, everyone, you should come, too, so we can work out where to survey tomorrow."

Only when they went outside, they found it was already snowing.

"Back inside! When this storm blows over, then we will search for Odin's army!" Karl shouted, brandishing his bottle.

THIRTY-NINE

The snow didn't let up for a week – so much for it being summer. No one was allowed to leave camp until the skies cleared, and while the others had endured this once already while Sibyl was down in the labs with Thor, this was her first time being confined to camp, and she hoped it never happened again.

The batteries on everyone's devices started to run down on the second day, and between the snow and the wall to wall cloud cover, the solar panels weren't much use for recharging anything. The gas cookers still worked, so they still had hot food and coffee, but that was probably the only bright spot in the whole week.

Well, that and Jorunn's bright idea to teach Thor to play poker. He grasped the rules readily enough, but the man had no concept of a poker face, and the better he learned to play, the easier it became to read his hand from his expression. It was probably a good thing they hadn't thrown gambling into the mix, or Jorunn would have robbed him blind. Poor Thor just couldn't bluff.

On the evening of the eighth day, Jorunn had endured an unusually bad losing streak, which meant it was her turn to go to the mess tent to check on dinner.

Jorunn returned quicker than usual. "I have good news and bad news," she announced.

Sibyl knew what she wanted first. "What's the bad news?"

Jorunn wrinkled her nose. "One of the guys was in charge of dinner, and he decided we're having smoked herring wraps with sauerkraut."

Sibyl felt bile rise up in her throat at the thought. What with being snowed in and having the supply run delayed as a result, everyone had been eating more, so they were down to the foods she liked least, and they'd had too much smoked herring to start with.

"Don't you want to hear the good news?" Jorunn asked.

Sibyl shook her head. "Nothing's good enough to make up for that."

"You don't know that," Jorunn said.

"What is it, then?"

Jorunn looked smug. "It's stopped snowing. If the skies stay clear, we might be allowed to start surveying again tomorrow."

Thor perked up. "Let me look." He made his way to the tent flap and stuck his head through. He just stayed there for a long moment, before he said, "She's right. There's a warm wind coming in from the ocean. It should blow this storm to the other side of the mountains, and melt all the snowfall in a matter of days."

"How would you know? Did you already sneak a look at the forecast while I was gone?" Jorunn asked.

Thor just shrugged. "My father taught me about the weather, and I'm never wrong."

The God of Thunder he wasn't, but he was as good a weather forecaster as whatever app Lara was using.

By morning, the snow had turned to slush, and the whole camp was a muddy miasma. By evening, Thor's promised warm wind had come to call, and within a day, it was like the snowstorm had never happened.

At dinner, Karl raised his bowl of baked beans in a toast. "Tomorrow, we resume our survey, and our search for Odin's army," he said.

He could have said they were looking for Odin's camp latrine pit, and they still would have cheered. Everyone else was too happy to be allowed out of camp to argue.

FORTY

By day's end, Sibyl's feet hurt from crunching over rocks, and if she had to lean over one more time to examine something promising that turned out to be nothing more than a freeze dried weed, she might scream. There had been some small finds in the area surrounding the pit they were all calling Odin's grave, but nothing like the dead army Thor had promised.

If she didn't know him so well, she'd have sworn he was lying about the other graves, but Thor couldn't even bluff at poker. If he said there was a whole company of ice mummies to be found, then the bodies were here somewhere.

"Who's on dinner duty tonight?" Karl asked.

"I am, with Jorunn," Sibyl said. She'd never been so grateful to be assigned to the kitchen in her life.

"You two head back to camp, then, and the rest of us will finish this last search pattern before it's too dark to see," Karl said.

Sibyl shouldered her daypack and trudged back to camp, hearing the scrunch of Jorunn's tired steps not far behind her.

"What do we have left?" Sibyl asked as Jorunn peered into the stacked boxes that were their makeshift pantry.

"Enough smoked herring to choke a whole pack of polar bears, and a box of dehydrated curry and rice."

Sibyl perked up. "How did we all miss that?"

Jorunn shrugged. "We're in Norway, not Australia. They're fans of Arctic fish, not sauce that'll blow your socks off."

Sibyl pulled out an armload of dehydrated meal packs and hugged them to her chest. "I don't know about you, but I could murder a curry," she quipped.

Jorunn grinned. "Pratchett, right? Academic humour at its best. Curry it is, then."

They both bustled about, emptying the curry packets into one pot and the rice into another. By the time they were ready to dish up, it was full dark outside, but none of the others had returned.

"Should I go get them and tell them dinner's ready?" Sibyl asked, looking longingly at the cooker. After eating fish for almost a week, the chicken curry smelled amazing.

"They know the way back to camp. They'll be fine," Jorunn said. "We should serve up while it's still hot. Let the others heat up leftovers if they're late."

After a week of sitting down to meals with everyone confined to camp, having the two of them at the table felt strange.

Sibyl had almost finished her dinner when she heard the squeal of someone unzipping the tent door. "About time. Dinner's probably cold by now," she said over her shoulder. She pointed in the direction of the gas cookers. "Help yourself."

"I have no need for sustenance. I came see that you are safe," Thor said.

Jorunn rose, dirty dishes in hand. "Well, that's my cue to leave. See you back in our tent when you two are done?" She dropped her plate and cutlery into the washing up tub and ducked outside.

"I'm a perfectly adequate cook, and I didn't cut or burn myself once tonight," Sibyl boasted.

"That is good," Thor said, peering out the tent flap. Only now did she realise he held his hammer with both hands, as if ready to strike.

A chill tiptoed across her heart.

"Thor, what's out there?"

"The witch and her protector. They came through the mountain pass just after the sun set, as your companions were leaving. Karl challenged them. He told them they were not allowed to be here, as it is a protected archaeological site."

Wow. For a man who didn't look entirely certain about what that meant, he managed to pronounce it pretty well.

But if what Thor had said was true, then this witch and her monster had cursed and beaten him in the past. If they were even slightly like Thor, they would not appreciate Karl giving them orders.

"What happened? Is everyone okay?"

Thor shook his head. "I do not know. She called to me, tried to summon me, as you did. I felt the call in my heart, trying to pull me away from you, but I did not answer. I will not answer. I am not hers to command. I am handfasted to you." He gripped his hammer even tighter than before, as though he feared this witch might try to take it from him. "She shall not have you. I will protect you. I will finally end the abomination that took my sister's life, and then I will force the witch to release me from this curse."

It sounded like a really good plan. One that might even work, except…

"Didn't you say the monster nearly killed you last time?" Sibyl ventured.

"Yes, but I have my hammer, and I know what I face this time. I will not be taken by surprise again!"

Even after a thousand years, the male ego was still as fragile as ever.

"Thor…"

How did one tell a Norse god he wasn't good enough to beat a monster? Not that Sibyl had ever seen this monster, but she did know he'd beaten Thor once. That was recommendation enough to avoid it forever.

"Thor, we must go." The second man to burst into the tent looked like a wirier, younger version of Thor. The man who'd handed her the satphone the other night, Sibyl realised.

"Not now, Loki. Astrid and Fenrir are here. We cannot leave until I have vanquished them both!" Thor snarled. He brandished the hammer at his imaginary foes.

Well, Sibyl hoped they were imaginary, or at least not close enough for combat. The mess tent wouldn't survive long if Thor meant to fight them here.

"You're a fool if you stay, Thor. Already I can feel the call. I've learned to resist, but it's only a matter of time before you answer. She will have you fighting for her, not against her, if you stay. Come with me. Together, we will wake Odin and the three of us will stand a far better chance against the witch and her pet. Together, we can beat them. Divided, we will fall, just as we did before."

Sibyl was inclined to agree with him. Then again, Thor had called him Loki, which meant he was a slippery trickster, every bit as devious as the movie character, if the myths were to be believed. Hell, wasn't he supposed to be Fenrir's father? A good father would do almost anything to save his son…

"What about Sibyl? I can't just leave her here at the witch's mercy!" Thor said.

Loki glanced at Sibyl, then just as quickly dismissed her. "The witch won't want any of these scholars. She wants warriors. She wants us. If we go to find Odin, she and her monster will come for us. We can't let her get to Odin first, especially if he still slumbers. We must wake him, and take a stand together."

Thor's eyes darted from Sibyl to Loki, as though he could not decide who to listen to.

Not that Sibyl had much to say on the matter. "I don't know much about fighting, but what I do know is that numbers matter. And strategy. If you stand a better chance of winning with allies, then you shouldn't fight alone."

Loki nodded, looking surprised. "She's wise, your little witch. You should listen to her."

Sibyl set her hands on her hips. "What did

you just call me?" She might be small, but no way was she letting some arsehole she didn't know call her a witch.

Loki smiled. "I called you wise. It means clever, an important quality in a scholar. Now, if Thor were even one tenth as wise as you, he'd see the wisdom of my advice, and we'd be halfway to Odin by now. Are you coming, brother, or are you determined to get yourself and your betrothed killed?"

Still Thor was torn.

But Sibyl had already decided. "Go with him. If I see your witch, I'll point her in the right direction of where to find you. I'll be fine."

Thor set his hammer down, so that he could take her hands in his. "Sibyl, promise me you will stay safe. I will seek out Odin, fight this monster, and get free of this curse. I will return for you, ástin mín. I swear it."

She believed him.

One kiss. Long enough for her to want it to go on forever, but too short for what might be farewell.

She might not like it, but she knew this was the right thing to do.

Thor released her, and raced out the door, with Loki on his heels.

Sibyl sighed. She wanted to shout after them to wait, that she wanted to come, too, but what good would that do? Loki might have called her a witch, but she was no more magical than…well, the stones beneath her feet. She kicked one, and it went bouncing off into the darkness.

What she really wanted to do was throw a tantrum of epic proportions. In the privacy of her tent, where no one would see. Where she could scream her frustrations into her pillow, at falling for a Viking warrior who might never come home.

The tent was empty, thank goodness. Jorunn must be in the bathroom, or something.

Sibyl picked up her pillow…

"Oh, thank fuck I found you. Quick, pack

your things, we have to go. Wait, not everything. Just enough for a couple of nights away. Pack light." Jorunn grabbed her backpack and began stuffing clothes into it.

"Where are we going?" Sibyl asked.

"With Thor and Loki, of course. You don't think those two can take care of things on their own, do you? Neither of them can operate a phone, or any form of modern tech, and they know next to nothing about our world. They need us, but we have to be quick." She stuffed an extra pair of socks into her backpack and cinched it closed, then zipped up her coat. She grabbed Sibyl's hand. "Come on, let's go!"

ABOUT THE AUTHOR

Demelza Carlton has always loved the ocean, but on her first snorkelling trip she found she was afraid of fish.

She has since swum with sea lions, sharks and sea cucumbers and stood on spray drenched cliffs over a seething sea as a seven-metre cyclonic swell surged in, shattering a shipwreck below.

Demelza now lives in Perth, Western Australia, the shark attack capital of the world.

The *Ocean's Gift* series was her first foray into fiction, followed by her suspense thriller *Nightmares* trilogy. She swears the *Mel Goes to Hell* series ambushed her on a crowded train and wouldn't leave her alone.

Want to know more? You can follow Demelza on Facebook, Twitter, YouTube or her website, Demelza Carlton's Place at:

www.demelzacarlton.com

Books by Demelza Carlton

Siren of Secrets series

Ocean's Secret (#1)

Ocean's Gift (#2)

Ocean's Infiltrator (#3)

Siren of War series

Ocean's Justice (#1)

Ocean's Widow (#2)

Ocean's Bride (#3)

Ocean's Rise (#4)

Ocean's War (#5)

How To Catch Crabs

Nightmares Trilogy

Nightmares of Caitlin Lockyer (#1)

Necessary Evil of Nathan Miller (#2)

Afterlife of Alana Miller (#3)

Mel Goes to Hell series

The Devil's Work (#1)

See You in Hell (#2)

Mel Goes to Hell (#3)

To Hell and Back (#4)

The Holiday From Hell (#5)

All Hell Breaks Loose (#6)

The Devil Goes to Heaven (#7)

Romance Island Resort series

Maid for the Rock Star (#1)
The Rock Star's Email Order Bride (#2)
The Rock Star's Virginity (#3)
The Rock Star and the Billionaire (#4)
The Rock Star Wants A Wife (#5)
The Rock Star's Wedding (#6)
Maid for the South Pole (#7)

Romance a Medieval Fairytale series

Enchant: Beauty and the Beast Retold
Dance: Cinderella Retold
Fly: Goose Girl Retold
Revel: Twelve Dancing Princesses Retold
Silence: Little Mermaid Retold
Awaken: Sleeping Beauty Retold
Embellish: Brave Little Tailor Retold
Appease: Princess and the Pea Retold
Blow: Three Little Pigs Retold
Return: Hansel and Gretel Retold
Wish: Aladdin Retold
Melt: Snow Queen Retold
Spin: Rumpelstiltskin Retold
Kiss: Frog Prince Retold
Reflect: Snow White Retold
Roar: Goldilocks Retold
Cobble: Elves and the Shoemaker Retold
Float: Enchanted Horse Retold
Steal: Forty Thieves Retold
Call: Pied Piper Retold

Feather: Swan Maidens Retold
Curse: Rose Red Retold
Cross: Three Billy Goats Gruff Retold
Weave: Rapunzel Retold
Claim: Puss in Boots Retold

Colony Universe

Cowboys and Aliens
Ghost
Vulcan
Cupid
Valentine
Prometheus
Halcyon
Poseidon
Apollo

Heart of Stone series

Broken Chains
Broken Bonds
Broken Dreams

Heart of Steel series

Stone Guardian
Stone Champion
Stone Sentinel
Stone Shadow